ON THE RIM

ON
THE
RIM

FLORIDA ANN TOWN

DUNDURN
TORONTO

Editor: Allison Hirst
Design: Jesse Hooper
Printer: Webcom

Library and Archives Canada Cataloguing in Publication

Town, Florida
    On the rim / Florida Ann Town.

Issued also in electronic formats.
ISBN 978-1-4597-0518-0

    I. Title.

PS8589.O957O5 2013   C813'.54   C2012-908615-0

1   2   3   4   5   17   16   15   14   13

We acknowledge the support of the **Canada Council for the Arts** and the **Ontario Arts Council** for our publishing program. We also acknowledge the financial support of the **Government of Canada** through the **Canada Book Fund** and **Livres Canada Books**, and the **Government of Ontario** through the **Ontario Book Publishing Tax Credit** and the **Ontario Media Development Corporation**.

Care has been taken to trace the ownership of copyright material used in this book. The author and the publisher welcome any information enabling them to rectify any references or credits in subsequent editions.

J. Kirk Howard, President

The publisher is not responsible for websites or their content unless they are owned by the publisher.

Visit us at
Dundurn.com | @dundurnpress | Facebook.com/dundurnpress | Pinterest.com/dundurnpress

Dundurn	Gazelle Book Services Limited	Dundurn
3 Church Street, Suite 500	White Cross Mills	2250 Military Road
Toronto, Ontario, Canada	High Town, Lancaster, England	Tonawanda, NY
M5E 1M2	L41 4XS	U.S.A. 14150

To Hugh, as always, and to Kat, Lyn, and Jenn.

Thanks also to my editor, Allison Hirst,
for her insightful comments.

— 1 —

ELLEN'S FINGERS PLAY WITH the worn gold band on her left hand, as if to confirm its presence. But the assurance is false, like so much else in her life. She should have stripped it from her finger two years, eight months, and five days ago, when her divorce became final. Or earlier, when Al walked out. Or when any one of a thousand things happened. But she didn't. Now she can't. Her fingers are too pudgy. She and the ring are locked together.

One of these days she'll do something about it. About the ring. About her weight. About her life. She turns her attention to a shopping list. She's learned to ignore the impulse items that once slid so easily into her shopping cart. Now she adjudicates her needs more carefully.

She glances at a group of young women walking through the mall. Their carefully made up faces radiate youth. Ellen runs her tongue over her lips, cruelly aware that her lipstick has worn off; her eyelashes, lacking a coat of mascara, are short, stumpy, and almost invisible.

She remembers a day long ago when she was their age. She had loosened her hair from its confining braids, the neat, tight braids she wore every day at school, allowing the tresses to fall over her shoulders in what she imagined was a cascade of shimmering beauty.

Her father had come into the kitchen as she helped her mother prepare dinner. "Your hair looks godawful. Do something with it."

"But everyone wears it like this."

"Not in my house, they don't. And if you're going to work around any food I eat, wear a hair net, like your mother does."

"But …"

There was no reasoning with her father, no discussion, and, as far as she could tell, no logic. Just pronouncements that came like bulletins from God.

"Fix it."

It was only one in a long series of arguments: the clothing she wore, the makeup she tried to use, the music she listened to — the list went on and on.

Ellen puts away the memory, turning her attention to a gaggle of school girls strutting past. Cropped tops clearly reveal nipples, unconfined by any type of bra. Jeans hang low on their hips, flaunting navels in front and buttock cracks in back. She wonders what her father would say if he were still alive. So much is bared today; he might have become accustomed to it. She snorts. No, there would be no chance of that.

Ellen squirms when one of the girls returns her gaze, but the flickering eyes weigh and dismiss Ellen in micro-seconds. She's relieved. She doesn't want their attention. The young people are compelling, complete and whole, with an intensity, a confidence and belief in themselves, that Ellen has never had despite a lifetime of matched cardigan sweater sets and colour-coordinated purses and shoes.

Her daydreams are interrupted when she catches sight of her reflection in the store window. It shocks her. Is that her face? With that thin little stretch of mouth? Carefully, so no one notices, she presses her lips together, takes a deep breath, and tries a smile. Somewhere, she read that F. Scott Fitzgerald told his daughter, Scottie, that the most important thing in life was a great smile.

Did he really say that? *Her* father never said anything about smiling. Only about saving money, doing chores, and turning off the lights.

Ellen thinks about the smiles that decorate the magazine covers at grocery store checkout counters. Julia Roberts, with her great, generous smile; Ellen couldn't smile like that if she practised for a thousand years.

"If smiles are so important, why don't they teach them in school," she asks herself. Startled looks remind her she's talking out loud. She rephrases the question in her mind. *Why not Smiling 101? Happiness 205? That should be more important than algebra.*

That night, she places her fingers on her cheekbones, pulling the skin back and up until it lies snug and tight against her bones. *I can have my face fixed,* she thinks. But her father's voice intrudes on her thoughts: "What's wrong with the face God gave you? What makes you think it would look any better if you had your nose stretched or your wrinkles stitched?"

Always, when her father was angry, he mixed his words. It enraged him if she laughed, setting off a tirade that mangled the language in truly spectacular ways.

"If Julia Roberts had a father like mine, she wouldn't have such a great smile either," she mutters to her mirror.

Her father wouldn't wear a seat belt. "You don't need one if you're a good driver," he once said. When he swerved on the highway during a snowstorm, the car flew off the road, killing both her parents.

An aunt took in her young brother. "Lloyd will be like a son to us," she declared.

But she didn't want the problems of a seventeen-year-old daughter. Someone else could take Ellen.

In a burst of rebellion, Ellen turned to the boyfriend her parents hadn't known about.

"Al, would your mother let me stay at your place, just until school ends?"

Al's widowed mother was dubious, but she found it hard to say no to her only child — and there was a spare room.

"Just till the end of school," she stipulated. But by that time Ellen was pregnant. She and Al got married right after graduation in a hurried and harried ceremony performed by a justice of the peace. Neither her aunt nor her brother attended.

Sighing, Ellen brings herself back to the present.

This place is so different from the home she and Al had built. Rented rooms don't smell like real homes. Teasing wisps of cookies or pot roast are replaced by the canned scent of air fresheners — a beige smell that matches the neutral paint on the walls. There are no yards, no gardens. That can be a good thing, or bad, depending. Poking around in the dirt and watching things grow is satisfying; other times it's a chore to cut the grass, weed the garden, and remember the times and days you're allowed to water.

Another memory kicks in.

"Al, it's four o'clock. Time to turn on the sprinkler."

"You do it. You're awake."

"No, I'm not."

"You must be. You know what time it is."

A symphony of sprinklers susurrates as she jams her arms into a dressing gown and stumbles outside, crossly cranking the water on just a little too much, warming to the knowledge that the *whump whump* of water hitting the driveway will keep Al awake.

In her fantasy, they always rush out together, tend the sprinklers, then return laughing to bed where they make passionate love. But it never happens. She yearns for the funny, spontaneous, warm and witty boy she knew in school. The man he became is more often cranky, harried, petulant, and dull. Like the lawns and sprinklers, her romantic dreams have washed away.

These days her interest in lawns and gardening is purely academic, like her interest in almost everything else. After the separation, she dragged her way through eighteen months of depression, when she literally didn't care if she lived or died. Her doctor's trial and error pharmaceutical experiments had brought dizzying ups and downs, alternating manic highs with hellish lows. Getting through each day was a major challenge, the simple mechanics of survival almost more than she could manage.

Her life is level now. No ups, no downs, no highs, no lows. Just dull. She's dull. Her small apartment looks dull. Utilitarian. Uninteresting. Uninspired. Unpacked boxes hunker in the corners of her space. She's forgotten what's in most of them. She still misses the easy familiarity of her home, where she didn't have to think about where things were, where she knew her way to the bathroom in the dark of night, the path down the hallway to the children's rooms, the route to the kitchen. Here, she stands for a moment before heading off in what she hopes is the right direction. Several times she's been jolted awake by bashing her toes into something she thought was somewhere else.

The front room contains one comfortable chair — enough, since she never has visitors — a bookcase, and a battered desk from the Thrift Shoppe that holds a small TV. A good reading lamp stands beside her chair.

The front room and kitchen are parts of an L-shape, with the shared centre designated as a dining area. Two chairs huddle around an Arborite and chrome table. Logic tells her that's all she needs, but there are days when she craves a larger table and many chairs, like her old dining room suite with eight side chairs, two arm chairs, a big glass-fronted buffet, and a table with extra leaves that invited her to spread out her craft projects in roomy splendour. Ellen's eyes have yet to adjust to her altered status.

I'll need extra chairs when the kids come, she tells herself each time she wanders through a furniture store in the mall. Then she looks at the price tags. What she has will do for now.

She rarely hears from the kids, and they've never come to visit; just the obligatory phone calls on Mother's Day, her birthday, and other mandated holidays. Judging from the talk shows she watches, this is a common complaint. In one way, she's relieved that the problem is general and not related specifically to her; in another, she's saddened that her children aren't the superior beings she thought she'd raised.

She tried brightening her apartment: Plastic placemats make red splashes on the table, gleaming wetly like spilled tomato juice. A brightly coloured dish towel hangs on a rack, its matching pot holders perch on the stove hood. The counters are woefully bare. No knick-knacks, canisters, or animal-shaped cookie jars clutter their beige surfaces. Her cupboards are equally bleak. A small fridge stands at the end of the counter; it holds little of interest, but its constant hum disturbs her sleep and scatters static through the radio broadcasts by day.

Her bedroom boasts a large, sprawlable bed. That was a mistake. The bed is comfortable, but its emptiness reminds her no one shares it. Matching night tables flank the bed, giving a sense of balance to the room. One holds a lamp, a book, a box of Kleenex, and her glasses, the other carries a clock radio whose green digital readout flips through the long hours of the night. At times she thinks about the contents of the night tables — photo albums that show her with Al and the children in earlier, happier days, a few birthday, Mother's Day, and Christmas cards from the children — nothing current. These are from childhood, when their printing wobbled across the bottom of the card and the words weren't always spelled correctly. Once saved, it seems disloyal to throw the cards out, even though she can't think of anything to do with them and rarely looks at them anymore.

Memories bang at the edge of her brain, like fat and sleepy houseflies, trying to force their way through window panes.

She hears the sound of Al's voice booming from the foot of the basement stairs, which was also the entrance to the garage. "I'm away. See you in a couple of hours."

"Okay," she called, without taking her eyes from the book. She sat, curled cozily in a corner of the chesterfield, the light of a reading lamp defining her territory. The gas fireplace hissed quietly, flicking flames through its imitation logs. The cat crept closer to the glass screen, intent on baking its brains until it went giddy with the heat.

Al was off to play racquetball. He was strong, active, and athletic. He loved the drive, the demands, and the quick responses that racquetball requires. He rejected Ellen's suggestion that he wear safety goggles.

"What's this?" he demanded when she gave him a pair as a birthday present.

"Sport goggles," she explained. "A lot of players wear them." She paused, frozen by his glare. "To protect your eyes," she added weakly.

"I don't need protection. I'm not some doddering old man who can't get out of the way."

Months later, she got a late-night call from Ben, Al's racquetball partner. They were at the hospital; Al had taken a ball to the eye.

"I can't believe this happened," Ben said when she arrived at the waiting room.

When Al dropped to the floor he smacked his head as well, so now he was in Emergency with possible occipital damage and a split scalp. A lumpy pad of gauze decorated the top of his head. Mercurochrome stained his forehead. An ice pack covered his eye.

"You're going to have a great shiner tomorrow," she told him.

"I know."

"Does it hurt much?"

"Not now. They gave me a couple of shots. You're looking pretty fuzzy right now."

"That's okay." She laughed. "I'm feeling pretty fuzzy."

He scowled.

She corrected herself, saying what she should have said in the beginning. "I'm so sorry. You don't usually have accidents."

There was a pause.

"What are they going to do?"

"Put a couple of stitches in my scalp. And look at my eye."

"Too bad you didn't smack your nose too," she quipped. "They could do a little plastic surgery at the same time."

His beak is a family joke. His father had a nice nose: inconspicuous, straight — the kind of nose politicians like because it doesn't lend itself to caricature. No one knows where Al's nose came from, but it's a generous-sized honker. He'd injured it a couple of times — once when he was young he broke it playing lacrosse and another time he didn't duck quickly enough during a boxing match. Still, it suits him.

"Don't make me laugh," he said, dismissing her attempt at humour. "It hurts when I move my face."

"Okay. Sorry."

A washed-out silence hung between them. The medicinal smell of the ward was mixed with other scents: dirt, sweat, grease, and things she couldn't identify. A cacophony of noise provided an urgent background. Pagers, telephones, and an overhead PA system competed with crisp commands from nurses, orderlies, and doctors.

"Is there anything I can bring you?"

"No. I'll be out in a couple of hours."

Silence again.

"I think Ben got my racquet. Call him and make sure."

"I will."

Al dozed off. Ellen wasn't sure if she should stay or go. A nurse walked in, writing something on a metal-backed chart. Ellen expected a white uniform, but the nurse wore a colourful cotton pant suit in a print that looked like children's pyjamas.

"We'll move him soon," she told Ellen. "We'll discharge him from ER and admit him to hospital."

She finished with the chart and hung it on the end of his bed. "You can take his clothes home if you want. He won't need them for a while."

"I thought he was going home in a few hours?"

The nurse smiled. "He'll be in for several days at least. He'll need reconstructive work."

"What reconstructive work?"

The nurse's face went blank. "I'm sorry, I can't discuss that. You'll have to check with his doctor."

That didn't match Al's version — that he'd be going home after a few stitches. But it was typical. He assumed that if he wanted something to happen, that's the way it would be. Better to let the doctor tell him. It would be one less argument she had to have.

Ellen walked back to the bed and gently touched his shoulder. "I'll see you tomorrow."

"Yeah. Okay. I'll let you know when to pick me up."

*

Racquetball marked a turning point in their relationship, planting the seed of a subtle grudge, but Ellen didn't realize it at the time. Al's idea of sharing an activity was for him to do it and her to watch. When he took up racquetball, he wanted her to come and watch. She did, reluctantly. She didn't enjoy it much. She didn't understand the game. There was a spectator's gallery, but it was more popular with teens as a place to hang out or sit in the corner and neck. Besides, it was hard to stay out late when there were young children to look after the next day. Ellen soon stopped going.

After the men finished their games, they used to stop at the bar to unwind, and it was usually one or two in the morning before Al arrived home. By that time, Ellen was in bed.

Did he blame her for not being there when he was injured? He never said. Luckily the operation went well. The eye socket was reconstructed and there was minimal damage to the eye. Before long he was back at work and returned to the racquetball court several months later. This time he wore goggles. The only reminder of the accident was a small scar at the corner of his eye that gave him a raffish Robert Redford look.

Ellen attended the end-of-season tournament, along with most of the wives and girlfriends. After, there was a big banquet where trophies were awarded and the players punched one another on the shoulder and told dressing room jokes.

In summer, Al played softball. When they were first married, Ellen went with him, loving the lazy feel of warm summer evenings. Not that she enjoyed softball. She found it funny: the catcher slipping sly signals from his crotch, the pitcher adjusting his jock, the players in their tight pants realigning themselves as they approached the plate. It reminded her of little boys at summer camp feeling the first stirring of their manhood, but caught in a cultural desert of self-denial that prevented them from celebrating their discovery.

Still, to please Al, she turned out for a few games, taking along a folding chair. There were no bleachers at the park where the amateurs played. And she kept a book in her shoulder bag.

"You might at least pretend to watch the game," he grated, after a strained and silent drive home one evening.

"What difference does it make? I thought you played because you enjoyed the game, not because of the spectators."

His breathing became slow and even — a metronome of anger.

"Other wives seem to enjoy it. They keep track of the scores and statistics. You should try it sometime. *They* don't complain about being bored."

"I'm not complaining," she said. "And you're wrong about the women. They talk about everything but the game. I can tell you who couldn't get it up last week after the game and who comes home horny. I just don't happen to be interested in listening to them. It's a treat to just sit quietly and not have to do anything."

"If that's all it means to you, go sit in some other park! You embarrass me."

So she did, walking to a local park with her folding chair and her book. Often there were Little League games in that park, and everyone assumed she was someone's mother. She smiled to herself when strangers tried to strike up a conversation by making observances about the game and she quickly learned how to deflect their comments and return to her reading.

It was a short-lived idyll, however. Paying a babysitter had been acceptable when she was watching Al play, but paying a babysitter so she could spend time in the park reading a book wasn't justifiable. And so she remained at home, first with Geoffrey, then the twins, Joanne and Jennifer, and finally Robby, the baby.

A crowded three-bedroom fixer-upper was all they could afford in the early years of their marriage, but when Al's mother died, the sale of her house gave them a good down payment on a tract house in a newly opened area. Ellen loved the house, but missed the convenience of the older parts of the city. There were no corner stores, no handy bookstores or coffee shops, just rows and rows of new houses, new lawns, and no fences. And women, behind the picture windows, coping with young children. It was a bonanza for the few teenagers in the subdivision, who were in hot demand as babysitters, but Ellen no longer needed their services.

Along with racquetball and softball, Al found time to join the local ratepayers association and was nominated for office.

"It's only once a month," he assured her.

Technically speaking, it was, but the subcommittees met frequently to prepare for those monthly meetings, and Al was on several subcommittees.

"What's so interesting about a ratepayers association?" she asked one evening as he got ready for yet another meeting.

"We have to do a great deal of planning," he informed her, in that "I know-you-can't-possibly-understand" tone of voice that he used so often in those days.

When Geoffrey was old enough to join Little League and Pee Wee hockey, Al tore himself away from the ratepayers to help coach Geoff's teams. When the girls were old enough for soccer, Ellen assumed he'd do the same, but he didn't. When it was Robby's turn for softball and hockey, he found time to coach again.

Ellen seethed, but felt helpless. She couldn't coach. She didn't have much contact with the other mothers and didn't feel she had much in common with them anyways; she wasn't part of the kaffeeklatsches. There was only so much dusting she could do, and once the children were all in school, the days lagged.

"Al, what would you think if I got a job?" she suggested over breakfast one morning.

"You've already got one," he said, refolding the newspaper and gesturing with his empty mug for a refill.

"I'm serious," she replied, quickly bringing the coffee pot to the table.

"So am I."

He broke the silence a moment later to add: "Besides, you can't do anything."

Several weeks later she tried again.

"Guess what, Al?"

A mumble from behind the paper indicated he wasn't into guessing games.

"I've joined the Noteworthies."

The paper drifted downward. "What in god's name are the Noteworthies?"

"It's a choir. We meet on Tuesday evenings."

The paper collapsed on the table. "I wish you'd said something first."

He sighed. The paper rose again.

❋

The choir was fun. They performed at care homes, offering Thanksgiving singalongs, Christmas programs, golden oldies, and gospel songs. They were a good choir with a repertoire of popular favourites. Ellen was proud to belong.

"We're singing a Valentine's Day program next week. Would you like to come?" she asked Al one night.

"No thanks. I can't sing."

"Other husbands come. And there's always tea and cookies after."

"Spending time with old people who drool and dribble into their bibs isn't my idea of a night out," he told her, his face frozen in distaste.

As the children got older, their demands increased and Ellen's Noteworthies were gradually phased out by service as a Brownie mom, Home and School support, Scout mom, Minor Hockey mom, and baker of endless cookies for various fundraisers. Sometimes the church held a bake sale and then she baked extra fancy cookies.

"Who are these for?" Al complained one night, helping himself to a krumkake. "How come you never bake anything for me?"

"Of course I do." She had laughed. "The cookie jar is always full."

"Those are for the kids. You never make anything special for me."

The next day she made a sherry-laced trifle for him.

"There," she murmured, piling whipped cream in luscious mounds, grating curls of dark chocolate on top. She gave the kids dishes of ice cream and presented Al with the trifle. He poked at it with his spoon.

"What's this?"

"It's trifle."

More pokes.

"Why can't I have ice cream?"

Wordlessly, she removed the dessert and replaced it with a bowl of ice cream.

Over the years, she evolved a mantra: "When the children are older, Al and I will have more time together." But it never happened. The kids went through guitar and accordion lessons, gymnastics, ballet, and karate. They played hockey and ringette, softball and soccer. They turned out for track and field and swimming lessons. Eventually they were old enough to get themselves where they had to be, whether by bike, bus, or carpool. Ellen joined a fitness class at the community centre; her interests hadn't widened, but her waistline had.

Summer vacations were unremarkable. Al was usually involved in a tournament, so family vacations were wherever the tournament took place. Three years in a row he used ten days of vacation time for international tournaments. These were solo events. The family stayed home while he went twice to England and once to Fiji.

"Here we are in Suva," he announced, after arriving home with a handful of pictures and some small carved turtles.

Except for the palm trees in the background, it looked like just another ball game.

"I didn't know there were women's teams, too," Ellen commented, looking at one of the pictures.

"There aren't," Al replied.

"Then who are all these women?"

"Oh, some of the guys bring their wives along — the ones who don't have families."

Later she learned they *did* have families, but the first wives and the kids had been left behind in favour of younger playmates who had their priorities straight and devoted themselves to their own personal "superstars."

*

But that was then and this is now, Ellen tells herself. No point in going over things she can't change — but some memories are hard to erase. After years of living with an absentee husband, Ellen is now officially "on her own." When the end came, it was more of a fizzle than a bang.

Al packed his bags one Saturday morning and announced he was leaving; his lawyer would contact her.

If it happened in a movie, there would be weeping, shouting, screaming, or even violence, maybe a pot thrown through a window or a lamp crashed against a wall. To her surprise, she did none of these things. In fact, she did nothing at all.

"Don't you even want to know why?" he had asked.

"If you want to tell me."

"That's exactly why — because you don't care. I'm tired of being nothing but a meal ticket. You don't care about me or anything I do."

"And someone else does?" she asked, with sudden insight.

"Someone does."

The room vibrated as the walls crowded in on her. Her brain buzzed, her throat tightened, and her gut cramped like it did when she was a kid and heard the whiplash of words her parents threw at each other; hard words, hurting words. She couldn't breathe.

She gulped a few times before she could utter a sound. Then she spoke, as evenly as she could.

"If that's the case, it really doesn't matter what I think, does it?"

"That's it?"

Her teeth grabbed the inside of her lip. She concentrated on her breathing.

"Thirty-two years and that's all you can say?"

She sat taller. "Thirty-three ... and I'm not sure what you want me to say."

Al glared at her. Whatever he expected, that wasn't it. "If you don't know, then I can't tell you."

Ellen's control evaporated. It was a line from one of the worst movies she'd ever seen, too corny to be believed. She repeated, half whispering, "If you don't know, then I can't tell you." Wonderful words. Every phrase book should include them.

Laughter bubbled up from somewhere, laughter that wouldn't be suppressed. It started with a quiver in her cheek, then a wriggle in the diaphragm. Finally, a snort at the back of the throat unleashed it and it escaped, ricocheting around the room.

"I don't see what's so funny." Al sulked.

"If you don't know, then I can't tell you," she gasped.

Finally, she got herself under control and looked at him, as a stranger might look at someone they've met for the first time.

He stood, flanked by his suitcases — poor, mute brackets surrounding his life.

"It's all right, Al. Really it is. Go. Have a good life."

His look would have shrivelled her, if she had cared.

"You are a cold-hearted bitch."

"You're probably right. Now, please, just leave."

"Not even a goodbye after thirty-three years?"

Ellen shrugged. "You're the one who's leaving. I'm not sure what you want. And at this point, I'm not even sure I care.

"Goodbye, Al. Does that make you happy?"

He swooped on his suitcases, opened the door, and stepped out. It was the kind of dramatic gesture he loved to make, but it needed a bigger audience.

Ellen knew reality would set in later, but she couldn't help laughing once again as she repeated to his retreating back, "If you don't know, then I can't tell you."

As she closed the door, her laughter rolled out, squeezed from the core of her being. This time she didn't even try to subdue it. After a bit, the laughter turned to tears, but she wasn't sure who or what she was crying for.

— 2 —

TWO DAYS AFTER AL'S dramatic exit, he had returned to claim possession of the house on the grounds that it was in his name. She'd thought of it as "their" house, but in fact he was the sole owner.

"You don't know how to do the maintenance or make repairs, or look after the lawns and all," he had told her. Nor could she afford the upkeep. He offered a monthly sum, enough, he said, to keep her in an apartment and to live on.

"It will be a lot easier for you," he told her.

Unquestioningly, she accepted, found an apartment and moved. She told herself it would be an adventure, but it wasn't. It was frightening. This was the first time she'd lived on her own with no one to rely on. No one to talk to. No one to turn to.

Her first night in the apartment had marked the beginning of a nightmare week of weeping and self-pity that gradually gave way to an envelope of deadness, muting her senses, leaching away her energy, and trapping her in a sea of lethargy.

Her boxes sat in accusing piles, forcing her to walk around them. She had neither the will nor the energy to unpack. She went to bed early, woke up late, and somehow passed the numb hours between with no memory of them.

Ellen drifted through the first few weeks and said nothing to the kids. But she finally realized she'd have to face up to it.

She stalled, dithering over the choice of paper. Fancy note paper didn't seem right. Plain paper seemed too ordinary. Finally she compromised, roughing out the letter on the ruled pages of an old scribbler.

Ellen watched the words scrawl crookedly across the page. She felt detached from the pen, from the page, from the letter. It was a ghostly feeling, as though someone else's hand was writing. She forced herself to focus on the line, re-reading it blankly.

I'm afraid your father and I can't work out our differences ...

Jabbing viciously, she scribbled the pen through her words. Stubbornly, they clung to life, refusing to be eradicated, forcing her to acknowledge their truth. She wished it wasn't so. She was still bewildered. She didn't know her marriage was in trouble until it was over.

Over. Over. Over. The words echoed in her head with the finality of a drum roll. Her chest felt paralyzed. She wondered if this was the first sign of a heart attack. Maybe that would change things.

But she knew it wouldn't. She wished there was some way to go back in time to a place where things hadn't yet begun to unravel.

She rolled the pen between her fingers, as though it might contain a secret compartment with happier messages. It didn't.

She started again.

I'm sorry to send you bad news.

"Why do I have to do this?" she muttered, rubbing her neck to deflect the probing fingers of a headache that niggled against the base of her skull, a ghostly hand picking at an unhealed scab. She shrugged off the notion that half of this problem belonged to Al and maybe he should be contacting the kids. It was easier to do it herself than to argue about it.

She had tried phoning them, but was crying before she had finished dialling their numbers. Wearily, she crumpled the page and watched as it dropped from her hand to the floor. Forget literary grace. Forget gentle phrases. There wasn't a pleasant way to deliver this news. She wrote bald, identical letters to each of the kids, slid them into the stamped envelopes, and trudged to the entry hall to drop them in the mailbox before she could change her mind.

Three days later, as though on schedule, they phoned, the calls coming within a few hours of each other. Geoffrey suggested counselling. Robby wanted them to stay with him while they "walked in the woods" and sorted out their universe. Joanne and Jennifer each suggested their parents take a cruise together.

"You need a second honeymoon," Joanne opined.

"Reawaken the magic," Jennifer offered.

Repeating the fiasco that passed for their first honeymoon would guarantee the split was final, but that wasn't something the girls need to know. Ellen thanked them for their suggestions and assured them no one had to come and help her.

Joanne, the most persistent of the children, phoned again and asked if she'd like to come and visit with her granddaughters for a while. Ellen knew it would be impossible to maintain a façade, to pretend that she was fine. Joanne has sharp eyes.

"Thanks, dear, but I've got a lot to do here. I haven't even unpacked yet."

"Are you sure you don't want me to come and help you?"

"No, I'll be fine, thank you."

Much as she hated talking on the phone, Ellen spent extra time with Joanne, to assure her that divorce isn't contagious — or inherited. She avoided talking about what went wrong. She wasn't even sure herself at that point, and Al's "if-you-don't know-then-I-can't-tell you" comment didn't bear repeating. She didn't mention the new "someone" in Al's life either. Unlike her let-it-all-hang-out children, Ellen had difficulty airing personal problems.

She talked briefly with Lissy and Jana, who danced before her mind's eye: elfin children who owned her heart — her only grandchildren.

"Guess what?" Ellen began brightly. "Grandma lives in a new house now. Maybe one day you can come and visit me."

"Does Grandpa live in a new house, too?" Lissy asked. Lissy, with the quick mind and bright eyes, the child who noticed things, picked up instantly on the fact that Ellen has said that only Grandma lived in the new house.

"No, he doesn't," she said, wishing for once that Lissy wasn't quite so intelligent. "Grandpa still lives in his old house — but we both still love you and you're our very, very favourite grandchildren."

Even as she said the words, she thought how modern it was. Single-parent homes and "theirs, mine and ours" households abound. Ellen wondered if *Star Trek*'s Seven of Nine, with her roots in a collective, wasn't a truer depiction of the future than Norman Rockwell's All-American family. No warm gaggle of cousins gathered at her grandmother's house, and it looked as though they wouldn't gather at Ellen's either. When her chicks left the nest they established their own lives, and Ellen was proud of them, happy for their independence, pleased with the people they had become. But there was an aching corner in her heart that still yearned for them and the grandchildren she so seldom saw.

During the months after leaving Al, Ellen had become aware of a piece of information which she decided *not* to share with her children. As "friends" had been quick to report, their father's girlfriend had moved in with him — moved in within days of Ellen's departure, in fact. The sheets didn't even get cool.

"She's not as young as she seems," one friend told her, her malicious enjoyment singing through the phone. "She dresses like my teenagers," another said. It was amazing how quickly they picked up information about the newcomer: Her name was Verna. She was foxy, blonde, lean, and a real fashion maven. She came from a place called Driggs, somewhere in Idaho. Ellen had never heard of it, but her friends seemed to know all about it. Verna worked as a cocktail waitress and had never been married. She smoked. She loved to dance. She quit her job when she moved in with Al.

Ellen wondered at the time if Verna wanted a family. Like a few of his buddies, might Al end up playing Daddy to someone half a century younger than himself? She wondered how her children would react. Children have highly conservative notions about parents' sexuality. A kiss, a polite hug, or some discrete hand-holding is tolerated, but anything beyond that is unseemly. Even the kiss has to meet certain dry standards. With few exceptions, such as Robert Redford or Warren Beatty, older people aren't supposed to tongue tango, especially not parents.

Unseemly or not, Al's girlfriend apparently staked out her territory in public with fully involved kisses, hugs, and bum squeezes. There was little doubt she had wedding bells in mind and the sooner the better. As one of Ellen's friends maddeningly reported, she wore the look of someone whose biological clock was not only ticking, but whose snooze alarm had already gone off.

Ellen had been wryly amused that no one supposed that she, too, might have met someone. Not that she had. But it was interesting that everyone simply assumed there wasn't anyone in her new life. They'd probably have been happier if she just joined a nunnery somewhere, if such things even existed anymore. Well, she didn't join a nunnery, but there were times since the divorce when she longed to be anywhere but where she was. Her lethargy frightened her. The dismal days when it was too much trouble to get dressed, too much trouble to prepare a meal, too much trouble to do anything were never-ending nightmares. She lived in her dressing gown, eating whatever was in the cupboard until it ran out and sheer hunger forced her to get dressed and go to the store.

The television played nonstop as Ellen slumped in her chair, letting whatever was on the screen wash over her and fill her days. One of those shows pointed the way to recovery by identifying her problem: clinical depression. It alarmed her enough that she finally saw a doctor. Not her own family doctor — she was too ashamed of what she had become to face him — but an anonymous doctor who had an office in the mall.

She worked through the desperate journey gradually, taking two steps forward and one step back. She couldn't be bothered with makeup. There seemed little point to it now that wrinkles and crow's feet had had a field day on her face. She tried to ignore her ballooning shape. Al's girlfriend might parade around in tight pants and skimpy tops, but Ellen camouflaged herself in sweat-pants and tops, shapeless and bland, in dark blues and blacks, telling herself that loose clothing hid her extra pounds. She knew she was lying to herself, but she couldn't face any more problems right then. One of these days, she promised herself, she'd get busy and lose the weight.

Gradually, she beat back the depression, and that in itself was worth celebrating.

Ellen now spends her afternoons in the Coquitlam Centre Mall, rambling through the stores. The food courts tempt her eye with richly decorated pastry, tantalize her nose with hot whiffs of french fries, and bombard her ears with the sizzle of teriyaki chicken hitting the grill, all accompanied by the whir of the milkshake machines. But mostly she enjoys watching the people. It's almost like television, but you can make up their stories yourself.

Beside the food court, a small display area features a chang-ing parade of entertainment. Today, there is a fitness promotion. Young men and women in shiny neon spandex bounce on tram-polines and turn flips in midair. Women with dandelion heads of blond hair ascend never-ending stairs. Clusters of spectators surround the demonstrations, watching a slender girl in shiny tights whirl the pedals of a stationary bike with a computer screen that shows rolling hills, while a well-muscled young man in a deeply cut tank top stands near her, lifting free weights. The erotic gyrations of aerobic dancers draw another crowd of spectators.

Beyond the main display area, just out of range of the ear-numbing music and squeals of the aerobics instructors, a small booth is tucked away. It looks lonesome. Out of curiosity, Ellen wanders over and finds the feature here is a row of bikes. In the background, a video shows groups of people pedalling off into the sunset along the Oregon coast, along the beaches of Santa Barbara, through the canyons of Colorado, and across Utah's slick rock trails.

Caught up despite herself, Ellen stops to watch the video.

Hah, she snorts mentally. *Why don't they show it like it is? With people riding along rainy city streets, soaked with spray from passing cars?*

Still, she has to give them credit for using ordinary people. They're reasonably fit, but not the overdone look of weightlifters or bodybuilders, just run-of-the-mill fit. She can imagine the people in the video stopping along the way at a Baskin Robbins for ice cream. They have the contented look of people who sleep in on Saturday mornings.

Watching the bikes, she remembers the feel of pedals under her feet and the wind blowing through her hair. She remembers the day she got her first bike.

"Happy birthday, Ellen." Mom was smiling as she slid a waffle onto Ellen's plate.

"Wow! We have a teenager in the family," her dad quipped.

Her brother, Lloyd, said nothing, but couldn't suppress a conspiratorial grin.

At last, breakfast ended and her father led her down into the basement, stopping at the foot of the stairs. He put his hands on her shoulders and turned her around so she was looking through the steps to the empty space under the stairs. Only that day, it wasn't empty.

"Happy birthday," he said.

A bike was leaning against the wall. The frame was shiny enamel. Fine lines embellished the silver fenders. A red reflector disc hung from the back fender and a shiny chrome bell perched on the right handlebar, ready for her thumb to bring it to life.

"But—"

Her father interrupted.

"I know. It's a boy's bike. You can share it with your brother."

Ellen looked again at the bike. It didn't seem quite so shiny, and the bell wasn't quite so appealing. He handed her a package, still in its store wrapper. Carefully she untied it. The paper fell away to reveal a light wire basket, gleaming silver, brand new, and just the right size to fit on the bike.

"Mine?" she asked.

He nodded. "You can put your schoolbooks in it."

Ellen didn't. It was usually too wet, or too foggy, or too something to ride the bike to school. Summer holidays were the best time. In the evening, parents drifted out to sit on their front porches, cooling off from the overheated kitchens where they'd just finished their dinners. Little kids played in front yards under their watchful eye. Older kids rode their bikes, wheeling them around in endless circles, weaving patterns along the road. Sometimes they pedalled a few blocks to a neighbourhood park, but mostly they stood, leaning on their bikes, talking away the endless summer evenings.

Ellen used the bike during that first summer. Then it became her brother's. She hadn't ridden a bike since, but on this day she watches the video twice, stands for almost half an hour as it plays through, then steps forward for a closer look. She isn't sure why she finds them so attractive. She certainly doesn't want a bike, doesn't need a bike, and has no intention of getting a bike. She's just curious.

"Can I help you?" The young man smiles — a friendly smile acknowledging her curiosity.

"No, no. I was just looking. They've certainly changed since I used to ride one."

"I'll bet you had coaster brakes."

Ellen nods in agreement. "Coaster brakes and a bell on the handlebars that you rang with your thumb."

"Look what they've got now," he says. His enthusiasm is infectious.

He urges her closer to one of the bikes. "Here. Touch this."

Obediently she presses her thumb to the black box fixed to the handlebar and literally jumps in shock at the sound that blasts from it.

"Great, isn't it?" he enthuses. "That's the loudest electronic bike horn on the market. It's a real safety feature."

His hands rove lovingly along the handlebar — a straight line of chrome, not the butterfly shaped bars she remembers.

"Look at this. It's a BLT rechargeable light — water-resistant, impact-resistant, and you can focus the beam down to a narrow pencil or open it into a flood.

"And here's the most comfortable seat you've ever tried. It's called an Easyseat. They've taken the nose off the traditional seat and separated the saddle so there's no irritation." His hands fondly pat two little pads that sit suspended over the centre post of the bike.

"I think I'd like something more traditional," she murmurs.

He nods in agreement. "I know what you mean. There are some really comfortable gel seats out now. Here's one you might like."

Ellen isn't sure how it happens, but she's suddenly perched on the seat of a braced bike, churning the pedals in brisk circles.

"See! It's just like they say." He beams. "Once you've ridden a bike, you never forget how."

He watches for a minute.

"Have you ever ridden a geared bike?"

She's short of breath by this point and doesn't want to waste oxygen on words. She shakes her head and concentrates on the task at hand, pushing the pedals around and around. Like ants around a dropped french fry, people emerge from nowhere to cluster around the display. Ellen feels their eyes appraising her performance. A tide of red washes across her face and creeps down her neck. A trickle of sweat rolls from vertebrae to vertebrae, gathering in a pool at the base of her spine. What is she doing, sitting here in the mall, making such a spectacle of herself? What if someone she knows walks by? What if Al walks by ... with his girlfriend?

Ellen wants to get off the bike but she doesn't know how. The young man is talking to others now. He's trying to make a living. Mercifully, he notices her distress.

"Here. You take a break and let me explain the gear levers," he says, handing her a folded paper cup of ice cold water. She accepts it gratefully, gulping it down. The back of her throat rebels at the sudden cold, sending shivers through her fillings and sharp pains into her ears.

He turns to the young men clustered around the bikes, explaining milk levers, derailleurs, front- and rear-geared wheels, and Shimano gear changers. Ellen doesn't know what he's talking about. He continues, with a loving description of Airstryke bars, which she can lean on for comfort during long uphill climbs or extended rides.

Long uphill climbs? She's not planning to do uphill climbs of any length —or any other kind of rides.

He plunges on, describing the wind tunnel advantage of cycling with the arms tucked in, like ski jumpers. "Boon Lennon discovered the aerodynamics of that one," he adds proudly.

John Lennon she's heard of. His music was part of her life. But Boon Lennon isn't even vaguely familiar.

As someone in the crowd asks another question, Ellen resumes pedalling, moving her feet in slow circles.

"It's wonderful, isn't it, that someone this age can stay young and still have fun biking," the young man is saying.

This age? Ellen doesn't consider herself to be "this age" yet. She's not exactly young, but being a tad past one's youth doesn't equate with "this age" except in the unfocused eyes of the very young. His words surround her.

"There's a seniors' bike club that goes from one side of the country to the other. They're even planning to go around Australia. We service their bikes for them. Some of them are in their seventies.... One is even in his eighties." He trots out this last fact with all the aplomb of a magician pulling a rabbit from a hat.

Ellen wonders idly if he thinks she's a senior. If she had enough energy she'd tell him that she's barely into middle age and senior is a long way down the pike.

Snatches of conversation drift by.

"Yeah — imagine having the time to make trips like that. Makes you wish you were ready to retire, doesn't it?"

He bends over another bike, answering technical questions from an athletic fellow who looks to be in his mid-twenties. Their hands fly as they share the esoteric language of gear ratios, aerodynamics, cadences, and super lightweight alloys.

At that moment, Ellen makes a decision. She steps off the bike and back into his field of vision.

"I'll take it," she says.

He looks at her blankly.

"The bike. I want it," she repeats.

"That's wonderful," he says. "I know you'll enjoy it. We can deliver it next week."

"No. I want it today. And I want it with a real seat — not that little pad thing. I want a seat I can really sit on."

"But ..."

"And take off that air horn."

The young man considers for a moment.

"Right. It's yours. I'll write up a bill of sale."

He turns to his associate and points to the bike. "Can you look after this for me? Take the horn off and change this seat for a standard gel?"

At that moment she realizes what she's done. She hasn't even asked how much it costs. A flush of embarrassment pulses through her, prickling its way up her neck and staining her cheeks. Quickly, before she can change her mind, she opens her purse and peeks in her wallet. Yes, the credit card is there.

He writes things on the bill while a scanner conveys information from her card to a computer in Chicago or some other distant place, which confirms that she has enough money somewhere to pay for the bike. This is her first purchase on her own card. As much as anything, she needs to prove to herself that she's entitled to use it. When she and Al separated, she didn't realize that after all the years of paying bills, all the years of looking after the household budget, their good credit rating was all in his name. She'd assumed it was a joint thing. She had a card with her name on it, but it turned out that was just a courtesy. It wasn't even that. It was pure sham. The account was Al's. Extra cards could be issued at his request, in any name at all. Later she learned that some people had them in the name of their family pet. Maybe that's what she was, a family pet.

Not until Al, on the advice of his lawyer, cancelled all the credit cards, did Ellen discover that everything she had was tied to him. Everything they'd achieved together turns up on the credit side of his ledger, but is totally missing from hers. It was a hard lesson.

She had to start from square one. To the business community, she was simply another woman with, as far as credit grantors were concerned, not much going for her.

Her heart pounds a ragged rhythm and anger builds at the memory. She's been afraid to use the new credit card. Someone might change their mind when they realize it's just Ellen and take it back.

At that moment the young man looks up, smiles, and announces the total.

"I'm giving you a demonstrator discount."

She smiles back and grabs the edge of the counter tightly.

He hands her something the computer has printed out.

She looks at it and nods.

He waits another moment before gesturing at the slip.

"You have to sign it."

Flustered, she looks down, grabs the pen, and signs her name. Then she thinks of something else.

"I'll need someone to help me get it in the car."

He's all smiles again.

"My partner will be right with you."

The partner, who has by now finished taking off the air horn and changing the seat, turns out to be as taciturn as his friend is garrulous, but at that moment Ellen is content to walk silently beside him. He makes his first comment in the parking lot, standing beside her car.

"No rack?"

"No rack," she affirms.

He looks at the car again.

"Let's try the trunk."

Quickly he opens the hatch of her Hyundai. He releases the rear seat back and folds it forward, opening the trunk to its fullest, then effortlessly picks up the bike and swings it into position. Try as he will there is no way to fit the machine into the back of her car.

"I'll have to take the front wheel off."

She looks puzzled.

"There's a quick-release lever on the wheel — see this thing?" His thumb presses a small chrome blade. "Push it like this to release the wheel. When you get home, fit the axle back into the fork and press the lever the other way."

He looks at her thoughtfully. She can feel him weighing her. Some sort of reading comes up on his mental scale and she lands on the good side of the ledger.

"Here. You try it."

He stands up, giving her access to the wheel.

It's on the tip of her tongue to say no, she can figure it out for herself, but she probably can't. She grasps the chrome lever firmly, takes a deep breath, and flips it. The wheel lifts out easily.

"Put it back," he instructs.

It's a little trickier to manoeuvre past the brake pads and fit the axle into its slot, but with a little juggling, she reassembles it and flicks the chrome lever closed.

He grunts approval as she steps away. "Just remember to double check it before you use the bike. Good idea to do it every time, whether you've loosened it or not."

He stoops, quickly unlocks the wheel, and slips the two parts of the bike into the hatch of her car.

"There you go, lady."

He pauses, then smiles. He has a nice smile.

"First thing I'd do if I was you is get a good helmet. Then I'd call a bike club and find someone to ride with. It's more fun that way. Safer, too.

"And make sure you check that wheel lock before you start to ride."

Quickly, he turns and walks away.

"Thank you," she calls. "Thank you very much."

He turns, smiles, and waves. "Good luck."

Ellen wonders if she should have tipped him. Everyone else seems to get tipped, and she's never sure if she's doing the right thing or not. But he's walked away so quickly that he probably didn't expect a tip. She hopes he didn't. People who want a tip usually waft around giving you lots of opportunity to slip them something.

He certainly hadn't done that, so maybe it was okay.

It has to be, she tells herself. *I can't do anything about it now.*

She thinks instead about her new bike, warming to the notion of riding it.

She prefers not to think about how he knew there was no one at home to help her with it.

— 3 —

GETTING THE BIKE INTO the apartment is worse than corralling a cat. What the young man swept so easily into the trunk transforms itself into an awkward pile of metal that refuses to co-operate in any way. Ellen's hands grip cold pieces of pipe, seeking purchase on the smooth enamel finish as she tugs it this way and that. Angrily, she lurches against the frame, twisting for leverage, and feels the sickening pull of a fingernail breaking below the quick. She pauses to blow a strand of hair from her forehead, where it dangles limply into her eyes, but finally manages to grunt the bike pieces from the trunk. Fitting them together costs her a scraped knuckle and another broken nail. Still, she feels a small swell of pride as she wheels the bike smoothly to the front door of her building.

There she meets another problem: getting inside. It takes two hands to balance the bike and one to hold the heavy door open.

"Shit!" she explodes.

Several frustrating minutes later she learns how to hold the bike steady with one hand, open the door with the other, jam her foot against the door, and back the bike through, leading it like a balky pony. At the halfway point she props the door open with her backside and guides the bike into the building by pushing on the seat and bashing her ankles against the pedals.

There are bikes on some of the apartment balconies.

"That means," she mutters, as she wheels toward the elevator, "that there has to be something better than this Monty Python routine every time I want to go in or out."

Before she can think about it further, another hurdle looms: the elevator. She walks the bike in, then backs it in. Neither works. She rams it toward the far corner but it refuses to co-operate. It's simply too big to fit in the elevator. In the end, it's easier to take the machine apart again. She feels like a mechanic by the time she reaches her apartment and reassembles the pieces, double checking that the chrome lever is locked in place before bracing the bike on its kickstand. If she wasn't so tired, she'd give up on the whole thing and take it back to the store.

Now that it's here, she doesn't know where to put it. Her hand caresses the smoothness of the handlebar. The tires whisper across the floor.

The apartment seemed empty when she first moved in, shouting for things to fill up its spaces, but the emptiness has evaporated. There isn't a convenient space for the bike in the bedroom or in the living/dining area. Briefly, Ellen considers storing it downstairs, in the locked compartment provided for each tenant, but she doesn't want to leave it alone in the damp and dark. And she isn't one of the lucky tenants with a balcony.

When the kids were little, bikes appeared in the front room only when they were under the Christmas tree. From there they went directly to the garage. Today isn't Christmas, and she feels guilty, as though someone is watching — a disapproving someone who will tell her bikes aren't allowed in the front room.

"I'm the one who washes and polishes this floor," she argues. "I can track across it in muddy boots if I want to."

She wheels the bike across the floor and stands it beside the window.

"There you go," she croons, standing back to get the full effect, "three-dimensional art."

The bike is compelling. It catches her eye unexpectedly. Gradually, the sense of surprise ebbs and she realizes she enjoys its presence in the room. It belongs here. And for the first time, she feels that maybe she does, as well.

※

It's several days before Ellen returns to the mall. The fitness demonstration has gone, replaced by a four-wheel drive white SUV, the dressed-up version of a Jeep, whose oversize wheels will likely never leave pavement, towing a metallic-flake painted boat — the kind that looks as though it's speeding even when it's tied up at a dock. Smiling young men try to entice passersby to buy raffle tickets for the car and boat, but business is slow.

Ellen winds past the display, heading for a sporting goods store farther down the corridor, looking for bike accessories. The open front of the store, fenced off by a waist-high wall of high-topped, high-priced running shoes, barely contains the energetic clerks who remind her of enthusiastic puppies, waiting for someone to play with them.

Sales staff, men and women alike, wear shorts, striped jerseys, and large, bulky running shoes that look forbiddingly expensive. As a group they give the impression they've dropped in on the way to or from the gym. As Ellen steps into the store, a young girl bounces toward her, oozing energy. Ellen hates her.

"I'd like to see something in a good bike helmet," Ellen announces. "It's for me," she adds, daring the clerk to smile.

"Right on," she chirps, unleashing such a friendly grin that Ellen feels like a Grinch for even suspecting she might have laughed.

A dozen helmets later they settle on a lightweight, well-ventilated model, which the girl helps her adjust.

"If it's too loose later, you can add these foam patches," she says, throwing a handful of charcoal grey squares into a bag. "Just peel the strip off the back and stick them on."

She glances at Ellen with concern. "If you haven't used them before, make sure you know exactly where they have to go. Once they're on, they don't come off." She fusses with the helmet, adjusting the chin strap, and confides, "I put them on with masking tape first. You're probably not supposed to but it helps get a better fit."

Ellen smiles, not sure why masking tape is frowned upon, but says nothing. The girl continues to fiddle with the straps before triumphantly passing the helmet to Ellen.

"There. That should be about right."

Ellen places the helmet on her head and reaches for the strap, but the girl moves swiftly.

"No. Not that way. Helmets don't sit on the back of your head. They have to come down on your forehead." Quickly she tilts it forward, until it sits over Ellen's eyebrows.

"There. Now do up the strap."

She waggles the helmet on Ellen's head. "Good. Nice and snug." But she isn't through yet.

"We've got a great special on bike gloves," she announces. "You'll like them. They've got gel inserts — way more comfortable than ordinary gloves."

The store has a full selection of bike wear too — body-hugging jackets and padded shorts, which the clerk insists are essential. Ellen zips herself into a jacket, wincing at the bright neon colour.

"Great visibility," the girl says.

Ellen agrees, but she's puzzled by a series of three pockets across the back of the jacket.

"No pockets on bike shorts. You need someplace for your keys and wallet. You can even put a spare water bottle in one of the pockets — or a Hammer Gel. That's a power gel — gives you quick energy. Great to have for the last lap of your ride."

Ellen slowly removes the jacket. Nice, but too pricey, she tells herself. Maybe later. But she will need shorts and squeezes herself into the largest pair of black shorts on the rack. The effort leaves her breathless. Quickly she peels them off, sliding back into her baggy sweats. As she leaves the change room, she notices a bulging book rack that covers every aspect of biking from repairs and maintenance to bike routes across the country and around the world.

"Fancy that," she muses, thumbing through a book about local bike routes in the Greater Vancouver area. In a spirit of abandon she also picks up *Biking in Ireland*. For "inspirational reading," she tells herself.

When she struggles into the new shorts at home, she decides a diet book would have been more appropriate. Her bulging butt is nothing to giggle at and shiny spandex does nothing to diminish it. Tomorrow, she promises, she'll take the bike out and learn to ride it. This evening she contents herself with straddling it in the front room, clicking the gear levers and adjusting the light, making diminishing circles on the wall, then expanding them out again. Someone (*Sammy Davis Jr.? Frank Sinatra? George Burns?*) ended his TV show by walking off the stage in a gradually diminishing spotlight until it, and they, were gone. From somewhere in the back of her memory she hears the theme song and hums along. "Ink, a dink a dink" — *of course! Jimmy Durante.*

The chrome handlebars look naked with only the small bell. Ellen reconsiders the electronic horn. She may get one. Today's traffic is neither as sparse nor as patient as when she was a child.

＊

The next morning Ellen walks the bike to a church parking lot that could have been designed for beginning bikers. Painted lines divide the stalls and there are no asphalt speed bumps. The lot is on a gentle incline, tilted just enough to allow her to work through the gears. Gingerly she sets herself in motion, pressing cautiously against the pedals, then more firmly as she gains her balance. At the bottom of the lot she pushes backward on the pedals to brake. Her feet spin wildly, meeting no resistance. A flutter of panic twists her stomach before she remembers: hand brakes.

Her handbook stressed using both hand brakes simultaneously. *Engaging only the front wheel brake while the bike is in motion can result in a forward somersault over the front wheel,* the book warned ominously.

Ellen wants neither a somersault nor a swan dive. Obediently, she squeezes both grips at once. The bike shudders to a halt. She turns it around, lines herself up with the other side of the parking lot, and tries again. Soon she can brake with relative comfort and security. Shortly after, she finds she can handle wide, swooping turns at the end of each pass across the lot and no longer has to lift the bike or walk it around in a circle to turn.

"Those are the basics," she gloats. "That's what everyone says you never forget. Now let's get into the new stuff."

She opens the book again. The instructions sound terribly complicated. They make even less sense when she tries to apply them. One set of gears is for the right hand, the other for the left, and she isn't sure what either set does, but there are two levers on each handlebar waiting for her thumbs to activate them. Warily, she pushes off again, building up enough speed to keep her balance, and cautiously presses the left hand lever. She's startled by a sudden *thunk* somewhere below her foot. Something has happened. She stops to look and realizes the chain is turned by a three-headed wheel instead of the single wheel she remembers from long ago. She clicks the lever again. Nothing happens.

"Dummy. It won't work unless you're moving," she mutters. She cranks the pedal and this time when she clicks the lever, the chain obediently jumps to the smallest wheel. She clicks the lever again but nothing happens. Maybe it isn't so simple after all. In desperation she pushes the second lever and the chain jumps to the middle wheel. After a bit of grating and grinding the chain jumps to the biggest wheel on her next push.

Happily, Ellen swings back and forth across the parking lot, changing gears first on one side, then the other, then in combinations. Gradually she realizes the differences between the two sets: big changes from the big gears under her feet, lesser changes from the little gears on the back wheel.

The bike book discusses gear ratios, which she understands in an abstract sort of way. She's not quite sure exactly how burning gasoline makes the wheels of a car turn, but she's grateful that it happens. She feels the same about the bike. She doesn't need to know how the gears work, only that they do.

She launches herself confidently now, straight up the steepest part of the parking lot, picking up speed, lurching through the gears until she reaches the top, swoops through a turn and glides back down, counting the *thunks* as each gear falls into place. At the bottom she gently squeezes the brakes and comes to an easy stop.

She reaches for the bottle mounted on the bike and sends a stream of water gurgling into her mouth. The taste of plastic spreads across her tongue and she makes a face as the water trickles down her throat. She should have soaked the bottle in something overnight.

She slides it smoothly back into its holder and contemplates her next move. It's time to graduate from the parking lot. Re-snugging her helmet, she adjusts the Velcro straps on her gloves and straddles the bike, pushing off smoothly, finding an easy rhythm as she pedals slowly toward a large industrial park nearby. Its wide, level streets offer a haven for a beginner. There's little traffic today and soon she's zigzagging happily from driveway to driveway, around buildings, up and down loading ramps, gearing up, gearing down, and sometimes, just for the fun of it, changing the focus on her light.

It feels wonderful. Ellen loves biking. She'll spend the rest of her life on a bike. Maybe she'll even sell her car and just use the bike. Become an eco-leader for women of "a certain age." She could design some trend-setting bike togs and become the Cheryl Tiegs of the bike world!

At that moment, in the middle of her dream, as she changes gears going through her turn, the bike suddenly lurches forward. Her feet spin in wildly ineffective circles. Frantically, she churns faster, then spins backward, but her pedals are unconnected. There's no resistance. She tries the brakes, thankful that they, at least, still work.

It's obvious that something has broken, but what? The bike is guaranteed, so she can get it fixed, but what to do now? She can't carry it home and she doesn't want to leave it here while she goes home for her car. She could push it, but the apartment is a good number of blocks away. Funny how much shorter distances seemed when she was riding. Briefly she wonders if there's a roadside service for bikers, with help for flats and towing and all that. Probably not.

Gloomily she presses the kickstand down and balances the bike against it while she drags out the biking book and sits on the curb, trying to figure out what's happened, trying to hold back tears.

"I should have known better," she rages. "Every bloody thing I try goes wrong."

She looks at the bike again, comparing it to the illustration that names all the parts. It's like the puzzles on the comic page: Can you see anything different in these two pictures? Then suddenly, she can. The chain hangs in a loose loop. Ellen searches through the index looking for something under "chains" or "repairs" or whatever else it might be hidden under.

"Chain come off, lady?" a voice asks.

She looks up. A young boy, eleven or twelve years old, leans over the handlebars of his bike.

"Chain come off?" he repeats.

"Yes. I think so. Yes, it did," she replies.

"Need a hand?" he asks.

"I guess I do. I'm not sure how to get it back on."

In a single motion the boy slides from his bike and drops it to the ground. No kickstand for him!

"Here. It's easy."

He bends over the rear wheel, presses something, lifts the back wheel and touches the pedal with one foot.

"There you go." He turns toward her, a triumphant smile gleaming across his face.

"What did you do? How did you do that?" she asks.

The smile disappears. This isn't the reaction he expects.

"This is my first time out," she says. "It's a new bike. If it does that again, I need to know how to fix it."

The smile returns. Someone has recognized his expertise. Even better, an adult has acknowledged him as an expert. He relishes the moment, carefully removing his baseball cap and replacing it firmly, visor twisted to the back.

"It's easy. See that little extra wheel at the back? That's your tension wheel. It keeps the chain tight. Just push that wheel and you can move the chain around and put it back on the gear wheel."

He doesn't often have the chance to instruct a grownup and he makes the most of it. The grin seeps over into his voice.

"Now, sometimes the chain doesn't come right off — it jams. Then you have to push it backward and loosen the tension wheel at the same time. When it comes free, put it back on, the same as before."

He steps back and looks at the bike. "Nice bike, lady."

He returns to his own bike, scooping it from the ground and lining it up beside him.

"Thank you," Ellen says awkwardly. "Thank you very much. I'd like to give you something, but I don't have my purse with me. Maybe you could …"

The youngster cuts her off.

"That's okay. You don't owe me nothing."

With another smile, he climbs on his bike and pushes off, pedalling swiftly to gain speed as he heads straight for a nearby curb and lifts himself and his bike over it, like the rider on a pure-bred jumper clearing the bars in a gymkhana.

That's a manoeuvre she'll try later. Much later. Or maybe it's a manoeuvre best left to the young.

Gingerly, she remounts and moves away. The chain stays in place. She pedals past the curb the boy jumped so effortlessly, and changes gears again. When she gets home, she'll try whatever it was he did to the bike. She can't depend on someone turning up every time she's in trouble.

"My knight in shining armour." She laughs. "Just my luck he turns out to be under-aged and riding a rusty old bike instead of a white horse."

She makes it home safely, releases her front wheel, and carries the two parts of her bike into the elevator and upstairs. She rejoins them and wheels down the hall into her apartment, then stands the bike back in its special spot by the window and searches her near-empty linen closet for a rag.

"All those years of saving stuff and now I don't have anything I need," she grumbles, thinking wistfully of piles of cleaning rags, plastic yogurt tubs, and brown paper bags stacked in her cupboards. Sighing, she assesses the skimpy contents of her closet and pulls out a pillow case. It's still too new and too good to cut up. She rummages further. There's a slightly worn dish towel with a couple of stains on it.

"You'll do," she tells it.

Ignoring the voice in her head that says there's still a lot of use left in the dish towel, she cuts it in half and rips one of the squares into smaller pieces. There's something exciting in the feel of the fabric and the resistance as she rips. She relishes the sound of shredding cloth. She uses one of the torn pieces to remove the road grime from her bike, another to polish the bike tracks on her floor, before squatting down in front of the bike to get into the serious work of finding out exactly what her knight in shining armour did.

Thumbing through her bike book, she discovers the technical term for her predicament: derailing. She derailed. For practice, she loosens the chain and replaces it.

"That's not so bad," she says, wishing a derailed life could be put back on track as easily. For now, she's happy to discover a new facet to her independence. She can fix a derailed bike. Suddenly, she's looking forward to tomorrow's ride. In her mind she sketches out a route that will take her down the highway, past the industrial area where she played today, and into new territory.

The next morning, Ellen has trouble making it to the kitchen. Muscles she'd long ago forgotten scream in outrage. Her tush refuses to speak to her. Parts of herself she can't even name vibrate with pain. Her new regime goes on hold while she hobbles into the bathroom and lowers herself slowly into the tub, hoping a hot soak will return a small degree of mobility and, if she's lucky, restore a modicum of comfort to a sorely tested area.

— 4 —

THE EXPRESS LINE NUDGES listlessly toward the register as Ellen shifts her basket, leaning it against her hip, trying to ease the dull ache that has invaded her shoulder. The elderly man in front of her peers into the basket he's balanced on the end of the divider rail. The line hiccups ahead, but he doesn't move. He's intent on re-checking his purchases, which are obviously over the express-line maximum of twelve items. Coupons bristle in his hand. Ellen sighs and glances at the young woman behind her. A wry shrug agrees with the unspoken comment: this will be a longer lineup than either had planned on. The woman's eyes flick to the next line, measuring the possibility of a speedier trip. She grimaces. This line is shorter, but will it be faster? Impatience hangs like a cloud around her head.

As though he hears their thoughts, the man turns, his face apologetic.

"I'm sorry to be so slow. My wife used to do all this. It isn't as easy as I thought."

"I guess most things look easy until you have to do them," Ellen agrees.

He smiles. A warm, friendly smile. A Grandpa smile.

"I wish I could take back all the times I complained that she took too long to shop."

"Mister, I wish my husband could hear you," the younger woman says, nodding her head vigorously. "That's about the first thing he says every time I come back from the store."

Slowly and carefully, he lifts each item from his basket and places it on the conveyor. One tomato, a green pepper, a small bag of mushrooms, a carton of strawberries, two bananas, and half a cantaloupe make a lonely parade down the centre of the black belt. He winces as the cashier bounces each item on the scale and whips it into the waiting bag.

Something from the bakery section is next. He watches anxiously as it's punched in. The next two don't cause any concern — soap powder is almost indestructible and the little package from the meat department isn't vulnerable.

The rest are coupon items — peanut butter, paper towels, eggs, cookies, a tin of soup (there is a brief discussion about whether he has the right kind), a small jar of jam, and a quarter-pound stick of butter. As he places each item on the belt, he shuffles his coupons like a deck of cards, searching for the right one, double-checking, then perches it on top of the container. They look like little birds sitting on a fence.

The goods scarcely leave his hand before they're whisked away, rung up, and bagged. The cashier's smile belies her impatience, but her thoughts are almost audible: "Let's get this in gear. I don't have all day and that lineup is getting longer." She'd be impatient even if there were no other customers in the store. It's the way of the young to be impatient with the old. She punches in the last item with a smile of relief and turns, waiting for payment, as the electronic scanner reads out the total.

"Thirty ... one ... dollars ... and ... sixty ... four .... cents" it says, with a disruptive mechanical pause between each uninflected word. "Thirty-one" and "sixty-four" are each read out as two separate numbers, not run together the way people say them in real life. Whoever recorded the numbers isn't the same person as the one who said "dollars and cents." The man's face registers confusion.

"I'm sorry ... how much is it?"

The girl's eyes widen in disbelief as she turns to read the numbers from her till display.

He apologizes again. "I have difficulty understanding machines when they read numbers. I know it's silly, but I can't make sense out of them. Maybe I need to get my hearing adjusted."

He pauses for a moment, and then laughs ruefully. "Maybe I need to get my mind adjusted. I'm not used to listening to machines and probably never will be."

At last the cashier's impatience registers and he reaches into his pocket for his wallet, carefully extracting two bills, slipping the wallet back into his hip pocket, checking that it's properly in place and buttoning the flap before reaching into his front pocket for a change purse.

"Sixty-four?" he asks.

She nods, her eyes lingering on the parking lot where a gaggle of teens cluster, the girls practising movie star stances while the boys studiously ignore them, shuffling their toes against the nose of their skateboards, sending them upward in controlled loops.

Carefully, the man counts out six quarters, a dime, and four pennies, lining the coins neatly on the counter beside the bills.

"Thank you," she responds, with all the animation of a Barbie doll, dropping the change into her till and returning the sales slip to him in a single gesture. "Have a nice day," she adds, in a manner as automatic and as meaningless as breathing.

"Sorry for the delay," she apologizes, smiling at Ellen.

"That's okay. I'm not in that much of a hurry. I wonder what happened to his wife that he has to do the shopping now. Must be quite a change for him."

The girl looks at the man's back as he shuffles toward the door.

"Died, I guess."

She dismisses the man and his wife and rings up Ellen's purchases swiftly and efficiently, as though demonstrating the way it ought to be done.

"Have a nice day," she says as she turns to the next customer.

The man stays in Ellen's mind, prodding her curiosity. There was tenderness in his face when he spoke of his wife. Fat chance Al would ever speak of her that way. But then, there's no catch in her voice when she discusses him, either. No hatred, no anger — just nothing.

Once there was passion and fire ... and love.

What happened? she wonders.

She remembers one special day — a day they worked together in the garden, tying up tomato plants and clipping off the lower leaves. Ellen's nostrils prickled with the pungent scent. It was a piercing odour that bore no relation to the way a tomato tastes.

"You go ahead," Al told her. "I'll put the stuff away."

She shed her clothing as she walked down the hallway, ready to step into the shower as soon as she reached the bathroom. The water was wonderful — warm and steamy, clean and refreshing at the same time. It tingled on her skin. Suddenly, the shower door popped open.

"Move over, Babe. Room for two in here." He grinned, lunging toward her.

They kissed, a soggy embrace that left them laughing as water streamed down their faces. They shuffled around, trying to keep the water from their eyes. He took the soap from her hand and gently lathered her back, arms stretching around her, pulling her closer, then turned his attention to her bottom.

"Nice butt," he declared, stepping back, then changing his focus, carefully applying lather and moving his soapy hands over her breasts. "I wonder what else we could do in a shower?"

They did.

He left and she was alone again in the steamy spray, savouring the gentle rasp of the water against her skin, still sensitive from his touch, his kisses and his nibbles.

It was hard to remember the last time they did something that spontaneous or that much fun. Somewhere along the line they ran out of steam, but Ellen can't recall when or why.

As she puts away the groceries, Ellen's mind goes back to the man in the store. He fascinates her. She tries to ferret more information from the brief encounter. What happened to his wife? Is she disabled? Is he now care-giver as well as shopper? She thinks again of the goods in that lonely parade — not enough for two people. Perhaps she had died. When a wife dies, it means a whole new way of life for her husband. But when a man dies, it doesn't alter the basics. Women have always shopped, cooked, and cleaned. They may do it with less money, but the tasks they perform are no different.

Still, Ellen muses, closing the crisper drawer, the hardest of all are the social relationships. Some women have skills that yield both money and an "office family." A few of her friends work, but none has what could be called a career, only part-time jobs that help cope with the cost of living. Just as important as the money is the sense of achievement, the chance to get out of the house and do something that someone values enough to pay for.

She stretches, rubbing an ache in her lower back, then opens the cupboard to put away the rest of the groceries. Tiny clusters emphasize how little is there.

Living on her own isn't a big deal for Ellen. She already knows how to cook, clean, and shop. Al has his girlfriend to look after these duties now, so he, too, has solved his problem. She wonders how good he'd be at looking after himself. Housework looks easy when you don't have to do it.

Grimly she smiles, thinking of all the times Al watched her do something, then launched, unasked, into criticism: "That would work better if you blah, blah, blah."

He had an inexhaustible fund of suggestions. She could never figure out where all this expertise came from, since, to the best of her knowledge, he'd never washed a floor, ironed a shirt, mended a sock, or cleaned a toilet — especially cleaned a toilet. His mom had waited on him in his childhood, and Ellen took over after they married.

The man in the store was different. He was doing his best to learn, not standing around being critical or waiting for someone to look after him.

She constructs a scenario for the man: His wife had a stroke a year or so ago and died soon after. He's in process of rebuilding his life. There's a family, of course. The children (she decides there are two, a son and a daughter, both married with teenaged families) live elsewhere. They want him to come and live with them. Their intentions are of the best, but he doesn't want to be a burden or interfere with their lives, so he stays here, on his own. He visits them once in a while and loves the time he spends with his grandchildren, but keeps his life separate from theirs. They fuss over him, write and call frequently to make sure he's okay, but lovingly give him space because they respect his need to be independent.

Ellen sighs, comparing the make-believe scenario to the reality of her own life.

"I wonder if he gets as lonesome as I do," she asks the electric kettle, gleaming mutely on the counter. "And I wonder if he gets as bored as I do."

Sometimes it's hard to remember what day it is. They blend, one into another, like watercolours running together on wet paper. She seldom goes out. The people she thought of as her friends were really Al's. She was Al's wife. Part of a couple. Al'n'Ellen, said like a single word. As a lone woman she no longer fits neatly into the barbecue and party groupings. Al and what's-her-name are now the couple and Ellen is the odd one out.

She doesn't care that much. Invitations create their own problems: it's hard for her to reciprocate. When they were younger, lack of furniture didn't matter. It was fun to sit on cushions on the floor. Now age-stiffened joints and added weight have changed all that. The floor is a lot farther away than it used to be, and the cushions aren't as soft. Beer and pizza generate heartburn and cause extra trips to the bathroom in the middle of the night.

Ellen thumps the cupboard door shut. When the children were younger, she'd have given her eye teeth for some time to herself. There were so many things she wanted to do, so many places she wanted to go. After the children grew, when she had more time, she still couldn't escape. You couldn't leave your husband and go travelling by yourself — at least not if Al was your husband.

Now she has no husband and no excuses, but lacks the ambition to pack up and go.

Her mind turns again to the man in the grocery store. How does he fill his days? She's sure he has lots of friends. Death brings friends closer. Divorce sends them running.

She constructs a typical day for him. An early riser, he makes a small, tidy breakfast each morning. Oatmeal, she decides, cooked in the same Pyrex double boiler his wife used. He cleans up his breakfast dishes before he goes into the yard to look after the small, tidy vegetable garden. He wears a cardigan sweater — grey heather. Leather patches on the elbows? No. A plain cardigan, she decides, carefully buttoned up.

After he finishes in the garden he visits with friends for a while. Maybe he works as a volunteer at a food bank somewhere. She wonders about his vacations. Does he always go "Back East" to visit his children? Probably. She knows many parents do that. She could, too, she knows, but she has other things to do.

Such as? There's that miserable voice in her head again. It's with her a lot lately, challenging and goading. *Come on,* it repeats. *Let's have some answers here.*

Ellen opens her mouth, then crossly shuts it. She doesn't have to answer. This is silly. She'd love to travel, for one thing. Everyone wants to travel. There are all sorts of wonderful places to go. Why can't she name one?

The television drones on in the background as the day drifts on, creating visual wallpaper and the illusion of friends and activities. She doesn't remember anything about the shows that were on earlier. She concentrates on the screen. There. She recognizes that place. It's in California. San Francisco. And there's another, farther south. Probably Santa Barbara. Poor old Los Angeles. It's never featured in commercials, just on the shows dealing with murder, drugs, or gang warfare; shows set in LA always have something awful happening to somebody.

Ellen finds the commercials more interesting, but even they get boring with repetition. Like the car commercial in the Grand Canyon that was once a knockout, now she's tired of seeing people and vehicles perched on top of improbable crags or driving up roads that look like ski runs in the summertime.

A talk show begins. They're the most boring of all. No action, no scenery, just people blathering away. Do they really do the things they say they do? And if they do, why talk about them on national television?

Her mind drifts. What would be the best way to see some of the places in the commercials? Not by car. When you drive you're too busy to really look around. Planes take you above and you never really see anything but a mosaic below: brown and green for countryside, a quilt-like grid of cement roads and rooftops for the cities. Perhaps a train? But trains only go along a narrow pathway? Bus? No, buses aren't ideal either.

Another commercial comes on. A young couple gallop

horses down a beach. She laughs. Most beaches have leash laws, pooper laws, or flat-out ordinances prohibiting dogs and other animals on the beach. She's pretty sure horses aren't welcome either, unless someone paves the way for the commercial with a generous contribution to one of the city's special funds. And cleans up after, with a shovel.

Horses might be an interesting way to travel. Just like the pioneers did, although traffic and urbanization would create problems. And if you check into a motel overnight, where do you put the horse? No, that isn't the solution either.

The program changes again. She's surprised when the commercials end and the late night comics come on. Abruptly, she realizes it's late and she's too tired to listen tonight. She hasn't decided yet if she likes any of the late night comics. She had a friendly (albeit electronic) relationship with Jay for many years on *The Tonight Show*. She still misses him and wishes the network would just play reruns of the old *Tonight Show*. Everyone else plays reruns and with all those seasons on file she'd die of old age before they started over again — or lose her memory and not recognize them as shows she'd seen twice before.

She switches off the set and moves to her end-of-the-day routine, slathering cream on her face, imagining the rich emollients soaking into her skin, plumping up the wrinkles and propping up the sags. She wears pyjamas now. She never used to, but they feel protective, like some kind of safety coating.

When the kids were small, it was a problem. If one cried during the night she had to put something on before hastily running down the hall. The children napped during the day, but at different times. One was wide awake at night while the others slept. They did a magnificent job of coordinating their sleep/wake schedules so they were never all sleeping at the same time. She grew dazed and groggy, yearning for an hour of uninterrupted unconsciousness.

Once, Al decided they needed a break and asked his mom to babysit. They set off like a couple of kids on a date.

"What do you want to do?" he asked eagerly.

She had no idea. They drove to a local park and tried to decide how to spend their precious evening out. She hadn't the energy for dancing; he didn't want to see a show.

"How about dinner?" he suggested. "We could go to Stuart Anderson's."

She shook her head. "I'm not that hungry."

The evening grew cooler and sudden shivers quivered across her shoulders. Al reached out and pulled her close, snuggling their bodies together the way they did when they dated, their breathing synchronizing, mutually warming and caressing each other. Suddenly they were teenagers again, isolated from the world in a darkened car. After, Al held her for a long while as she slept, cuddled in his arms.

It was almost midnight when she awoke. "We'd better get back," she stammered.

"Yeah, you're right," Al agreed. "Silly as it sounds, I really enjoyed this."

She rearranged herself on her side of the car while Al started the engine and pulled away. Driving past the local theatre he suddenly stopped, opened the car door, and ran over to the entrance. He bent over, picked something up from the ground, then rushed back to the car.

"What's that?" she asked.

He grinned. "Our passport. Mom's going to ask what we did this evening, right?"

She nodded.

"We'll tell her we went to the movies — and here's the ticket to prove it."

When they got home, Al casually laid the ticket stubs on the table as he talked with his mom, thanking her for babysitting.

Her eyes took in the tickets and accepted them, and as she turned to get her coat from the hall, Al winked at Ellen. Moments later, one of the boys began to cry and Ellen scurried off to soothe away a troubling dream.

✳

Ellen presses her thumb against the ridged wheel of the thermostat, turning it down as she does every night. She can twirl it until her thumb falls off, but it never seems to make a difference. She suspects the thermostats are little more than window dressing to keep the tenants happy while the real temperature is controlled in the caretaker's apartment on the main floor. She turns it up in the morning. Sometimes it warms up and sometimes it doesn't. It likely depends on what time the caretaker gets up and adjusts the real thermostat.

As usual, sleep is slow to come. The apartment isn't restful. The building is noisy — not the raucous people-party noises or the hum and whir of machinery, but the more sinister and inexplicable night noises of boards that creak and groan, things that crack and bang, and unidentifiable sounds that whip her into heart-shuddering wakefulness, unsure of what snapped her from sleep, but knowing a return to restfulness is out of the question, at least for a period of hours, if not the rest of the night.

These are the hours when Ellen has ongoing arguments with herself. Should she take sleeping pills to get through the night? Lack of sleep is tough enough, but it's even harder to slam awake each night, sipping in shallow breaths of air and hoping she survives until the safe hours begin around 4:30 a.m. when the bad things go away. If she survives until then, she falls asleep easily and stays asleep until traffic noises wake her later in the morning. The problem is getting through the hours between midnight and the blessed hour when the hobgoblins go home.

Okay, so I take a sleeping pill, she tells herself. *So then if there's any trouble, I'm drugged and can't respond. I'll get my sleep but it might cost me my life, or who knows what else.*

She knows, but won't admit her fear. Not even to herself. She doesn't want to bring back the memory of the nights her father came into her bedroom. Or the shattering time her mother discovered them and raged at Ellen: "How could you let him do that?" But her mother never told an eleven-year-old Ellen how she could have stopped him.

She shivers, closing the door on the memory, groping for peace, fighting for calmness. There has to be a way to get over her fears, but she isn't ready to admit to anyone what a sissy she is, or to discuss the things that terrify her. She reads articles by health gurus who claim everything can be solved with proper nutrition and exercise. She tries their programs, working out when she remembers, eating potassium-rich foods, swallowing stress-proofing vitamins, and drinking herbal teas until they come out her ears. Well, not quite her ears. The net effect of four cups of night-time tea is burping. Later the ructions move farther down her digestive tract. At those times, she's glad she sleeps alone.

She'd hoped riding her bike would help her sleep. Now that she's more confident, she regularly rides to the library or the store, on errands involving items she can tuck in her backpack. An hour-long trip no longer leaves her exhausted, but she still can't sleep through the night.

Wearily, she continues her lockup rounds. Wooden lathes cut to size drop into the channels of the sliding windows. She checks carefully to make sure the stove and the TV are turned off before walking into the bedroom and closing its lockless door. She jams one end of a short one-by-six under the door and raises the other end of the board by propping it on a book — Hedley Donovan's *Right Places, Right Times* does nicely. A wedge of wood would be a neater solution, but she doesn't have one. A bag of empty tin cans hangs from the bathroom window, which swings out over the alley. *If anyone touches the window, I'll hear them in an instant,* she reassures herself.

She picks up the bedside phone and listens to the reassuring buzz of the dial tone. *Two seconds to call 911 and summon help if I need it.* She repeats the number, relishing the feeling of safety and security it engenders.

As she lies in bed, waiting for sleep to come, her thoughts return to the commercials she watched earlier. Where would she like to go? What would be a fun place to see? She knows the answer before she can form the words. It's a feeling, more than a specific place. It's a mixture of sunshine, warmth, sea breezes, and sand: a visual impression of brilliant flowers and sun-bronzed people. Somewhere in California.

So why doesn't she go? What's keeping her? Certainly not a job; she doesn't have one yet. She has enough to pay for the apartment and cover basic living expenses, plus a small emergency fund.

Maybe this is that emergency, she thinks. Why not? Who says emergencies have to be unpleasant? Emergencies are events that come up quickly and require sudden action. She decides she has an emergent need to go to California. All she has to do now is figure out where and when … and how.

Rolling out of bed, she tugs the book and board from under the door and heads for the kitchen. A warm drink might help. This is the perfect time to try the decaffeinated coffee mix she bought on impulse weeks ago and hoarded, waiting for the occasion that never happened.

As she steps through the doorway, a ray of light shoots in the window. Where it comes from, she doesn't know, but it lands smack on the new bicycle and stops her in her tracks.

"Of course!" she whispers. "That's why I got it. I'll ride my bike to California."

As quickly as the thought arrives, her uncertainty evaporates. A feeling of peaceful purpose fills her and a snuggly feeling of contentment surrounds her. The more she thinks about it, the more appealing it becomes. She wriggles with excitement, moves rapidly into the kitchenette to plug in the kettle and bring down the bright red tin of Swiss Mocha powder from its shelf, spooning it into her special cup. She can almost feel the road beneath her tires. If it wasn't so late, she could start tonight. Then that damned logical voice intervenes again.

Oh, no, you couldn't, it says.

Okay. Not yet. But soon. Soon, she promises herself.

The cheerful hum of the kettle announces it's almost ready to boil. Plenty hot enough for her coffee mix. Ellen fills her cup to the brim, watching the light brown granules float on the surface and the milky foam blend its way through the mixture. The drink is no longer consolation, it's celebration. The rich, brown taste of mocha coffee slides down her throat and ricochets through her system, bringing warmth first here, then there.

She picks up the bike books and riffles through the index. Her luck holds true. Nothing in it refers to California. Hopefully, she flips through the pages, checking out listed tours, just in case one of the maps might show the Pacific coastline. None do.

Sighing, she returns the book to its spot on the shelf, searching for an atlas before realizing that she knows exactly where it is. Just where it's always been. Back at the house in the spare bedroom bookcase. Not much of an atlas — they'd bought it years ago when the kids were in school. It wouldn't be much use in any case. Atlases fall out of date with increasing rapidity these days.

"Just like cars," she says out loud, laughing wryly. "A new model every year."

Over the years, the African countries changed their names, the Middle East revised things, the British Commonwealth broke apart, the South Pacific fractured, and Europe reassembled itself with all new pieces and new players. Russia disintegrated and provided the world with half-dozen new countries that were actually old countries, whose names no one could spell, say, or remember. She strains to recall some of the old names — Rhodesia, Ceylon, and Zaire. A fuzzy contingent lurks just beyond reach of her memory. It reminds her of an old Danny Kaye routine, and she tries saying them, scat style, mangling the names. Then she grimaces, remembering something else. Danny Kaye did the routines but it was Sylvia Fine who wrote the clever material that catapulted him to stardom. Sylvia Fine, the invisible wife.

She sighs. She doesn't have an atlas here, but she'll look at one tomorrow at the library.

Ellen glances at the stove clock. Somehow, it's almost 4:30 — time to turn in again. Relieved, she knows she'll have no trouble sleeping now.

And she doesn't. She doesn't even dream, or if she does, she doesn't remember.

One thing she does remember: California and the bike. In the brilliant rays of the morning sun the bike looks newer and shinier than ever. She peers in the mirror. She definitely doesn't look either new or shiny. She looks old and haggard and tired. Very tired.

Wearily she picks up the coffee cup, holding her hands under the running tap water, watching bubbles form on her wrists as she rinses it out, rubbing away the crusty brown circle around the rim.

What a silly idea that was, she tells herself. *Imagine thinking someone my age could do such a thing.*

She looks again at the bike. The sun glances off the shiny paint, twinkling at her in invitation. A dare.

"Oh, come on," she tells it. "Would you really want to go on a trip like that with an old fogey like me?"

At that moment, the sun reaches the shiny chrome nut centring the handlebars. A splash of light cuts, with laser-like precision, into her eye. She's taken aback. It's as though the machine is trying to communicate with her. Or she with it. "Get a grip," she tells herself. "Next thing you know you'll be parking under a crystal. Or maybe a triangle."

She giggles at a sudden thought. "Maybe it's a Harley Davidson that's come back as a Nishiki."

Struck by a sudden impulse, she steps to the bike, raises her leg and straddles it. It feels good. The saddle is no longer strange — it's a comfortable friend. Her fingers fall readily into the subtle indentations on the handle grips. She clicks the hand brakes, watching the small square pads on the front brake clasp themselves along the rim of the wheel.

Maybe it isn't such a silly idea after all. Maybe she could do it. Maybe she could at least find out a little more about it before dismissing the idea completely.

✳

"Okay. First stop, library," Ellen tells the bike later that morning, after carefully taking it out into the corridor, down the elevator, and edging her way through the door. As she pedals away, she's awash in good feelings.

"This is a wonderful idea," she says. "It isn't silly. I'm not too old. I can do things by myself. Al can go take a flying leap. I don't need him anymore."

The wheels purr happily as she pumps along, the tinkle of street gravel hitting the inside of the back fender punctuates the sound of the tires, creating something that's almost music. The click of the chain drive adds an undercurrent of rhythm and she smiles. A lightly scented breeze rushes playfully along. The sun adds a benediction. Somewhere inside her mind music bubbles up: "California, Here I Come." Corny? Well, yes. But what the heck. If she's going to be eccentric, she might as well enjoy it.

For a brief moment she thinks about the kids, then tells herself to forget them. They won't approve, but she doesn't need their approval. She doesn't need anyone's approval anymore. Ellen nods her head. Her shadow echoes the motion, her helmet enlarging her head, making the move even more emphatic.

Another song inches into her mind. "What a Wonderful World." She listens to the familiar lyrics in her mind, hearing Satchmo grind them out. That's more like it. Anyone who's going to ride a bike to California is entitled to happy thoughts. And damn it, she's going to get what she's entitled to.

The wind sings gently as it whispers through her spokes.

It *is* a wonderful world.

— 5 —

IT'S STORY TIME AT the local library. Little kids slump bonelessly on the floor, giggling as a ventriloquist removes a book from the shelf and converses with its characters. Mothers drape themselves against the wall, enjoying the chance to do nothing. Ellen unfastens her bike helmet and pats her hair into some kind of order.

A quartet of women at a reading table nibble at conversation: mice gathering crumbs from yesterday's words. Their eyes swing toward Ellen as she enters, measuring her like scanning devices at the airport. They are a neatly matched set. Each is the colour of well-done toast, the generic snowbird complexion that looks like plastic masks in the joke shops. Their jersey tops fit snugly to show slim waists, while sleeves mask their flabby arms. Each has a short, fluffy hairdo in some shade of Clairol and wears party makeup: eyeshadow, liner, and blusher. Lipstick creeps in lines and runnels around their shrivelled lips.

Ellen feels naked. She hasn't worn makeup for years.

The polyester glee club is polite about her aberration. They don't frown or stare openly, only a flat, sideways sliding of the eyes that registers the rolls in her spandex shorts and her dishevelled hair. Like ripples through water, a subtle lip quirk circulates around the table before they return to their conversation. They don't laugh or even smile, just that light flex in the wrinkles around their mouths before they dismiss her.

She feels diminished. Resolutely, she trudges through the tables, making her way to the in-house computer. Hesitantly, she brings up the travel category, adds *guide books* and *California, Oregon*, and *Washington* to her search. The computer whirs and churns, creating the illusion of busy fingers inside the machine, flipping through files and catalogues as small people scurry around searching industriously through miniature lists.

Their search is successful. They produce several promising titles. Ellen jots the numbers of one of the little pieces of paper that sit in hopeful stacks near the computer; recycled paper, not good paper. Or is recycled paper now the better kind of paper?

Dewey decimals send her to the right section and the right shelf, but the aisles are too narrow. Can't blame Dewey for that. Nor for the fact that she forgot to bring her glasses. By the time she stands back far enough to read the titles on the book spines, her bum is in the middle of the row of books behind her. *I've pressed spines with some of the world's best authors,* she thinks.

She builds up a stack of possibilities, flipping through pages at random. The library limit is fifty titles, so she decides to take them all — all the books in her stack. Nine titles, not fifty. She laughs at a mental picture of someone staggering out the library door with fifty books in a pile. *Does anyone ever take the limit?* she wonders.

Story hour is winding down. If she doesn't check out soon she'll end up in a mob of knee-high lenders as the kids grab armloads of books. Ellen wonders how many actually get read. Her kids used to come home from the library with stacks of books, too. They'd read about three, then ignore the rest until a thin film of dust muted the colours on the jacket of the top book. She could have either nagged them about taking the books back or take the easy way out and do it herself. It usually became her chore, largely because if she didn't take them back, she was the one who had to pay the fines. Was there an obscure clause in the

Children's Allowances Act that prohibited using allowances for things like library fines? The howls that greeted her suggestion one day that they pay their own fines made it seem that way.

"That's not fair," Jennifer muttered. "We can't take them back unless you drive us to the library, and you didn't."

"You didn't ask," Ellen countered.

"We've got a game on Saturday," Robbie mumbled.

"We do too," Joanne added.

Four pairs of eyes focused glumly on the books.

Ellen gave in.

"All right, I'll take them back. But this is the last time."

She probably should have insisted. It would have been a cheap lesson on how the world works: builds character; generates good habits. It would also have set off a tempest of whines. Ellen hated coping with the monumental sulks that followed when the kids were forced to do something they didn't want to do. Looking at it another way, it was a small price to pay to encourage literacy — if that was what was actually happening.

She's knocked out of her reverie when the librarian reaches for her books. Ellen fumbles for her library card and places it on the counter, barcode up. The red light of a computer pen flashes over it and a machine whistles encouragingly as the librarian slides the pen over the bar code on the outside of the book, then lifts it to pass the spine of the book over a pad that neutralizes whatever it is that sets off the exit door alarm on unchecked books. The new system may be efficient, but Ellen hates it. She never knows when the books are due back. She wishes they'd go back to the old system of stamping a date on a slip pasted on the inside cover of the book and making friendly conversation while they did it.

Outside, Ellen juggles the books into her saddle bag, snuggling them together tightly so they won't bump her leg while she pedals. Then she unlocks her bike and re-wraps the chain.

The lock is Kryptonite. She used to think Kryptonite was a name made up for Superman comics and was surprised to find it was real stuff. She's still not sure it's an actual element, but who knows?

Ellen mounts the bike and pushes off, heading for home. Her muscles feel good now. She pictures them sliding smoothly over one another as she pedals along. They seem to be happy muscles. She feels the pleasure they get from a workout. Do muscles sweat? The top of her head is warm under the helmet and there's a damp spot forming in the curve of her lower back. She can't keep Kleenex in the middle pocket of her bike jersey. It gets soggy with sweat.

She slows for the traffic light, flashing amber, then red, and pauses to pull her water bottle from its holder, enjoying a fast drink. She used to feel embarrassed drinking from it in public — too much like a baby bottle. Now she doesn't care. It's quick and it's easy. If anyone thinks it looks funny, that's their problem, not hers. Her body is specific in its demands now. When she works out, it wants water, and wants it frequently. There's a trail of water bottles in her apartment. One waits in the fridge, ready for reading or TV watching. Another sits on her night table.

Is it possible to become addicted to water? Everything else seems addictive. People used to have a "bit of a sweet tooth," but today, they're chocoholics. She wouldn't be surprised if there was an association to help them kick their habit; CA, with its own twelve-step program. Athletes get high on endorphins when they work out. Nicotine addicts plug in a different set of chemicals.

Ellen muses on a group to deal with "aquaholism." She pictures herself, seated with fellow aquaholics, in a dimly lit room. Voices come clockwise around the circle. Soon it will be her turn.

"My name is Bernice (she'll use a fake name), and I'm an aquaholic. I snuck a drink from the fountain in the library while the librarian thought I was looking at books."

The light changes and she slides the red, domed bottle back into its holder. She sees it from the corner of her eye, as images sneak in where they don't belong. The cylindrical shape poised under her crotch looks like a huge plastic penis. She squints until it turns into a harmless water bottle again, then pedals off.

Her mind wanders while she rides. Her thumbs control the gear levers almost automatically now and her eyes swivel from side to side, checking the traffic ahead, beside, and behind her in regular sweeps, like the swing of a windshield wiper. She wears a little rear-view mirror on her helmet — the kind that looks like a dentist's mirror and gives a glimpse of what's coming up behind. It makes her feel safer.

All this happens with no conscious thought, and the churning rhythms of her quads and calves take her to another level of non-thought. She feels like a passenger on the bike, no longer involved in what's happening.

Ellen watches things along the side of the road. Shoes. There's a story about all the shoes beside the road. They're all supposed to be left shoes. She never had time to check it out before, but there's time enough when you're on a bike to check out everything you see. They aren't all left shoes. Oh, wait! They're *left* — as in *left behind*. How dumb can you get? All this time she thought they meant left shoes, as in right and left. That's funny. She'll have to share that with the grandkids. See if they get it or, like her, think there's a legion of unmated right shoes sitting around somewhere waiting for the other half of the pair to come home.

There's lots of broken glass along the roadside, along with a few pop cans and beer cans. And plastic bottles, like the ones that hold dishwashing soap. Where would those come from? Surely no one walks out to the car with an empty soap bottle to dispose of beside the road?

The detritus of the roadside fascinates her. Bolts, screws, and metal washer rings are scattered like confetti. They range from truck-size to Smart Car–size. She expects them to be rusty, but most aren't. She pictures them falling from obscure engine parts and dropping slyly by the road bed. Do their owners ever figure out what's happened? Do gangs of black-market mechanics sneak around in the middle of the night, scooting on their backs on those little dollies, sliding up and down rows of parked cars, loosening bolts so the engines will fall apart?

Snarls of tangled audio tape line the highways. She read somewhere that there are 250 feet of tape in a 90-minute cassette. Is that true? Does anyone ever re-roll these miles of tape and replay them? Which artists stretch the farthest along North America's highways? How many cassettes does it take to go from coast to coast?

Used Pampers line the ditches. Ellen corrects herself. She can't say that. Pampers is a trade name and they might be other brands as well. To be politically, socially, and "advertisingly" correct, she has to say "disposable diapers."

Whatever. They clutter the roadside. Now that she thinks about it, she can't remember ever seeing a cloth diaper beside the road. What does that say about people who use cloth diapers and people who use disposable diapers?

On a more grownup note, there are lots of shirts beside the road. Mostly men's T-shirts. Some look quite new. She has a quick flash of a young, hunky muscleman taking off his T-shirt, putting it on the roof of his car, and flexing his pecs for the benefit of passing motorists. He's so hyped by his own exhibition he drives away and leaves the T-shirt on top of the car, to blow off and join the roadside collection.

Other things appear — sheets of loose-leaf paper, scribblers — but no books. She's never seen a book thrown out beside the road. She has seen lampshades, though. And garbage cans. Probably from do-it-yourself moving ventures; pickup trucks pressed into service as low-cost mini moving vans, with odd, lumpy shapes pressing out against billowing tarps. Sometimes tarps wind up beside the road, too.

She's leery of the cardboard boxes that squat defiantly in the middle of the lane, daring drivers to touch them. Most won't. They swerve around the boxes, then glance in the rear-view mirror. The empty mouth of the box laughs at them. The boxes pose a hazard for her. Drivers will swerve to miss the box and hit the biker on the side of the road. Sometimes the box is beside the road and she has to cycle around it. She always touches it with her foot to see if anything's in it.

Boxes on the road remind her of a horrible story she read about in the newspaper — someone put unwanted kittens in a cardboard box and dropped it on the highway, where a semi-trailer ran over it and killed the kittens. Witnesses said it was lucky there were no children playing in the boxes or they would have been killed. Wasn't it bad enough as it was? Those kittens actually died. They weren't hypothetical deaths. Besides, no one would put kids in a box and dump them on the highway, would they?

Something about pedalling sends Ellen's mind into a strange, hypnotic mode. Long-forgotten memories drift up from the bottom of her mind. She talks with people, repeats conversations, and revises responses. No one can hear her. It feels good.

Sometimes she talks to Al, but not often. They ran out of things to talk about long ago. Maybe that was part of the problem. He talked and she listened. Or at least she looked like she was listening. They used to enjoy reading the Sunday morning paper together. After breakfast, she'd clear the table and Al would hand over a section of the paper to read while they enjoyed a second (or third) cup of coffee.

She couldn't remember when he'd started reading things out loud. It was sweet at first. He wanted to share things with her. Then it changed from being a commentary about an item to reading the whole story and grew until it seemed like he was reading the whole paper out loud. She was expected to make a response, so she had to listen. She felt like telling him it was difficult for her to read her section of the paper with him reading out loud. It also spoiled the stories for her when he handed that section of the paper over. There was nothing left to discover.

At least she doesn't have that problem anymore. She can read her paper in any order she wishes, without having to listen to someone talk at the same time.

What makes her think of that now? Perhaps the pages of newspapers lying beside the road stir up that particular memory.

Sometimes she talks to the kids while she's riding, rehashing some of the old arguments. She laughs. Even with all the wisdom and culture she imparted, none became a Nobel Prize–winner. Probably just as well. Ellen's fond of them just as they are.

Lately she's been going farther back in her memories, dredging up bits and pieces, things that still scare her and skulk on the borderless shadows around the edges of her mind. The truth is, she feels really ratty today. Biking isn't fun. Reading isn't fun. Nothing is fun today. She's still upset from this morning. On the way to the library she passed the squashed body of a squirrel lying on the road. It couldn't have been very old, probably just a few months, and must have been killed several days ago. It was stiff and dry and leathery-looking, with hair that stuck up in clumps. Its mouth was open, as though in an "O" of surprise when the tire ran over it.

Why doesn't someone move it off the road instead of leaving it there for everyone else to run over? Why didn't she move it off the road? She couldn't make herself touch it. She didn't even stop. Now she's ashamed of herself.

"If it's still there, I'll move it," she promises.

But she "accidentally" takes a different route home.

— 6 —

THE NEXT MORNING, ELLEN'S mind is filled with left-over dreams, strange, disturbing dreams. Not indecipherable surrealist images, but dreams filled with everyday things. In one, Ellen opens a door and their pet cat, Gulliver, runs in meowing and brushing her ankles, just as he used to. She feels the whispery-soft touch of his fur against her shins and her ankles tense as he passes by. She hears him meow with her outside ears, not the internal sound of dreams. It is so richly sensual, so real and so persuasive that she expects to find Gulliver sitting under her chair, waiting to be fed. She's disappointed when she wakes and he isn't there.

It's a beautiful day. There isn't a cloud in the sky, but even that doesn't make her happy. She doesn't want breakfast. She wishes she still smoked. There would be comfort in the long, slow morning drag that used to open each day. Ease in watching the curling rings of smoke, the pleasant sensation of the cigarette between her fingers. A cigarette would bring her head back into focus. Her breath releases itself. It's been years since she bought a pack of smokes, so there isn't even a leftover butt to snipe. Ruefully, she opts for a ride, hoping to clear her head. Even as she pulls on her biking clothes, she knows the cigarette would have been better. Easier. More comfortable.

When she finally sets out, the air is fresh and cool. Not cold, but cool. Birds chatter in tight rows along the telephone lines.

Whatever it is they're talking about, they're so deeply engrossed in conversation that someone riding by, which ordinarily whirls them into the air in huge panicky flocks, drawing pictures against the sky as they wheel and change directions, doesn't register today.

Ellen's disappointed. It's wonderful to watch their swirling and swooping. How do they know when to turn? Somehow they do, and all wing over at the same time. They're much better than human drivers. They don't crash into each other and wipe each other out. They don't have feather benders, or skyway pileups. There's no air rage, no shaking of beaks and claws, no mid-sky collisions as they charge against one another, squawking and shrieking with anger.

Her tires give a reassuring *shush* as she pulls up at an intersection, waiting for the traffic light to go through its choreographed sequence: left turn, amber arrow, green light, amber light, red light, left turn. The control box on the corner clucks before each change, like a broody hen deciding which chick to hatch. This crossing doesn't have the audio signal that lets visually impaired persons cross. The audible traffic signals make different sounds. They chirp, bleat, cuckoo, beep, or whistle. She wonders how it would feel to face traffic with no vision. It must be frightening. Still, the different audio warnings must be confusing. She wonders why no one has standardized the sounds of safety.

Traffic isn't building yet. The few cars that go by are driven by people delivering newspapers or other things. Whatever happened to milkmen? Vegetable trucks? Paper boys? She remembers boys at school with paper routes. They hung out at the paper shack, after school, members of a select fraternity. No girls allowed. No hangers-on. Only boys, with their hands swirling rapidly over piles of fresh newspapers, folding them into hard rolls that they tossed, like batons, onto front porches as they wheeled smoothly by on their bikes. There are no paper boys now, only adults servicing routes in cars, with hundreds of papers to deliver in the early morning hours before most working people are awake. Who knows, she may soon be forced to find that kind of job. What seemed like sufficient money when the divorce settlement came through has dripped away at an alarming rate. She puts off buying things and is bitterly aware that her life is on hold. After struggling through the divorce, the depression, the rebuilding, things should get better. But the cosmic plan hasn't kicked in yet. Instead, her rent is going up, and the utilities are following suit.

She's still replacing things in her kitchen. Every time she wants to make something it seems she has to buy something to make it with, on, or in. Muffin tins, cake pans, microwaveable containers. The list goes on and on. It's time for a new tradition: showers for the newly divorced to help them replace a lifetime of accumulated goods.

The residue of tension left by her dreams evaporates as the sun warms the day. Traffic thickens, almost unnoticed, like pudding just before it comes to a boil. Time to get off the road before the air turns solid with exhaust fumes and the noise level blots out the hum of her tires against the pavement.

Starbucks, near the mall, opens early. Ellen decides to treat herself. It's too early in the day for the jolting infusion of an espresso. She pictures a latte, heaped with frothed milk, dusted with cinnamon and raw sugar.

Briefly, she thinks about buying a special coffee maker so she can have a latté whenever she wants. It would save a couple of dollars every time she used it. Crossly, she dismisses the thought.

"That's government thinking," she tells herself. "Spend two hundred dollars to save $2.50." Unlike the government, she has to either pay her bills or go bankrupt. This thought jolts her back to her original problem. Sooner or later she has to make a decision. What kind of job to get? What kind of work can she do?

She still has a little leeway, a little stretch of freedom ahead of her, but it's evaporating rapidly.

She takes her latte outside, sinking gratefully into the green plastic chair that's already absorbed comfortable warmth from the sunshine. Business people pass by, gulping their coffee as they head for their jobs, walking toward the still-locked doors of the mall where security guards inspect them before granting the minimum of open door required to get in. Others wait impatiently for coffee to go, in specially shaped mugs that slip into the cupholders of a car. Their shared deadlines generate a sense of camaraderie. This isn't just a coffee shop, it's a club to which they all belong.

Ellen isn't a member. She's grittily aware of her bike clothes, in contrast to their office outfits. She's in running shoes while they wear the latest, modish shoes. Beautiful boots. Stylish shoes.

Sighing, she picks up a discarded newspaper and glances through the pages. The business section has been removed. She looks at the other tables. The business section is definitely the thing to read if you're a member of this group. *Forget it,* she tells herself, crossly. Soon enough she'll qualify to sit here in her status shoes and read the business pages. Today, she relaxes and enjoys the sun against her legs while she savours the cinnamon on her latte.

There's a little rush away from the coffee shop. Time to open the offices. Time to ready themselves to meet customers. Time to start the day. Like flights of little birds that whirl in midair on some invisible command, the coffee drinkers respond to a signal Ellen doesn't hear.

The busboy comes to clear the tables. He eyes her for a moment, then clears around her. Deftly. Silently. The silence triggers her memory. Why should silence bring back the memory of an argument?

They were in the bedroom. Not for anything as interesting as sex. They hardly ever used the bedroom for that anymore. She was doing something mundane, like putting laundry away.

Ellen doesn't remember why Al was there. It wasn't important. When she finished, she began making up the bed — straightening the covers, pulling the sheets tight, and fluffing the pillows.

"You know, that's one thing that really annoys me," he stated, with no preamble.

"What is?"

"The way you make the bed."

She stopped to look at him.

"You mean like I'm doing now?"

He shook his head, a mean, grimy little gesture.

"No. Like what you *aren't* doing now. All you ever do is straighten it. You only make it when you put clean sheets on the bed."

She didn't know what he meant.

"I don't understand. Are you saying you want me to put clean sheets on the bed every day?"

He exploded in anger.

"There you go again. You never listen to what I say!"

"You're wrong," she said patiently. "I'm listening as hard as I can. I can hear your words, but I can't understand what you're trying to tell me."

"What I'm saying is that you never make the bed. All you do is *straighten* it."

"That's something different?"

"It's a lot different. My mother used to make the bed properly every single day."

"So tell me how she did it."

"She took all the blankets off, took the sheets off, and shook them outside, in the sunshine, so they went back on the bed smelling nice and fresh. Not all stale from somebody sleeping in them."

Her mind started to giggle. She did that when the boys were younger and their beds smelled of old running shoes and farts. This didn't seem the time to share that information.

"Does the bed smell stale to you?"

"Oh, forget it." He spat the words out.

"No, I'm serious. Is that why you're telling me this?"

"Just drop it. I don't want to talk about it anymore."

He stalked from the room, leaving her standing beside the bed, one corner of the spread in her hand, ready to flip over the blankets. She was confused. Now that he had worked himself into a snit he'd be angry if she unmade the bed and did what he wanted. If she didn't make it properly, he'd be resentful.

She stripped the bed. She'd change the linens. It would be an excuse to make it "properly" without triggering another round of argument.

Sitting at Starbucks, enjoying the sunshine, with the taste of latte coating the inside of her mouth, she can't believe that argument actually happened. Nor can she believe she responded as she did. She gropes inside her mind, looking for a word to describe her behaviour. There isn't one. What do you call someone who's afraid to make a statement, any kind of statement?

It was different from the quarrels her parents used to have. Those were bitter, harsh battles that went on and on into the night. When the bickering started, Ellen would freeze, cramps clawing at her stomach. It was dangerous to do or say anything that might call attention to herself. Fear stalked the room, waiting to throw her into the fire of their anger.

She never knew how to talk things over with Al. All discussions aren't arguments, are they? What would happen if she'd said what she really thought? Most of the time, it probably wasn't worth raising the question. Like making the bed. Was that something really worth fighting over? Or was it the excuse for something else? Was there something he wasn't naming that was fulminating inside?

She shakes her head. It's confusing and unsettling. She hates herself for a lifetime of spineless behaviour. The constant caving in, placating. Being eternally wrong. What would she do today if the situation repeated itself? The honest answer is, she doesn't know. She really doesn't know.

The busboy returns. He wants to clear the table. She glances at her watch, surprised at the time.

"Sorry," she says, pushing back her chair.

"That's okay. It's nice out here," he replies.

She walks her bike across the highway, in the pedestrian lane. Maybe she'll stop at the library on the way home and see if there are any other books about bike trips. She mounts and pedals slowly, enjoying the feel of her foot against the pedal. It's a nice, solid sensation. She's pleasantly surprised that it doesn't feel like exertion anymore. Her muscles don't burn and scream and her lungs don't gasp and wheeze.

The handful of cars in the parking lot confirms that the library is open. She parks the bike, locks it carefully, and pushes the door open.

The same four women, in the same polyester track suits, sit at the same table. *Do they live here?* One catches Ellen's eye and smiles, nodding her head slightly. Was this what she took for a sneer last time? Ellen can't imagine what was wrong with her. They look like perfectly nice, friendly old ladies, wearing perfectly nice, practical clothing. Ellen returns the nod, smiles, and walks to the computer.

The books she'd hoped to get haven't been returned yet. Should she look for something else to read? She spends a lot of time reading lately. Why is that? She was always an omnivorous reader but these days she consumes books at a frantic rate. She hears her daughters' voices in her head.

"Get a life, Mom. Get out and do real things with real people."

It was good advice several years ago when they first said it. Maybe it's still good.

So, what sort of real thing should she do, and which real people should she do it with? It's a pleasant puzzle that Ellen rolls around in her head, savouring the options open to her.

And what, that voice interrupts, *are those options?*

There's always a job.

Right, the voice agrees. *With the highest unemployment level since the Recession and with your wonderful work record — that single year of weekend clerking while you were in high school and nothing since — there's probably a line of employers just waiting for you to walk in.*

So, okay, getting a job might not be that easy.

She dismisses the problem. She's not ready to tie herself into a regular schedule just yet. It's one reason why she hasn't looked for a volunteer job. She's done lots of that. It's great stuff. Good for the community, good for the individual. There are lots of advantages to volunteering, but she's not ready for that kind of commitment either. And it doesn't help pay the bills. What Ellen really wants to do is take some time for herself and do something totally outrageous.

She wants to ride her bike to California.

All the books from the library, all the maps, all the videos have stopped being daydreams she teased herself with. It's become something real, with a texture of its own. *California.* She rolls the word around in her mouth, tasting it, feeling it. She's suddenly serious about the trip, more serious than she's ever been about anything.

After she does it, she'll go on and do whatever she has to do. But not yet. Just this once she wants to do something for herself. Something no one will approve of. She knows that already. So she won't tell anyone. There it is again. Why such fear of disapproval? No one is writing a report card about her; no one except herself. And she's not ranking herself very highly.

Ellen thinks again about her daughters' comments. *Get a life. Find some real people.* Easier said than done.

Her parents had moved a lot, so almost every year she went to a different school. Each year, Ellen's mother repeated the same litany: "You'll make new friends in no time."

But she didn't. All through her school years, she met other children, learned their names, and became acquainted with a few, but they never became close friends. It was as though they had built-in radar that warned them not to invest in this friendship because it wouldn't last. And it didn't. At the end of the year, they inevitably moved again. At the next school, she saw other girls walking together, talking in the private shorthand of long-time friends. But that closeness eluded Ellen. She never walked with someone in that way, nor talked with someone in that way.

Growing older, she discovered it was easier to find new boyfriends than make girlfriends. Boys could present a problem, but that was easier to deal with. If a boy was too persistent, she dropped him and found another boyfriend. Her parents didn't want her to become involved with boys, so she never mentioned them at home.

In her early teens, she did go to a few parties. Her father would delivered her to the door and call to pick her up at 10:00 p.m. She was pinioned on her embarrassment when he turned up at the door, stepping inside the front hall to wait for her. Just standing there, he cast a pall on the evening. She left, not when the party ended, but when he thought she should be home.

"Please, Dad," she begged. "I can come home with someone else. And it isn't far to walk."

He shook his head, adamant, angry.

"Ten o'clock is late enough for anybody. And nice girls don't go walking the streets after dark."

The summer Ellen turned sixteen, her mother offered to throw a birthday party for her. It was a great idea and Ellen was full of exciting plans. But no one she asked could come to the party.

"I'm not surprised," her mom replied. "Most people are busy during the summer. Families go away on vacation. And some of your friends are working." She busied herself with the meal she was preparing, leaving a long pause before adding, "Never mind. We'll have a party later in the year, when everyone is back in school."

Ellen wonders why she suggested it in the first place if she didn't expect anyone to come. They moved again. Ellen didn't know anyone at the new school. The party was never mentioned again.

When she met Al, they hung out with his friends.

"You'll like them," he told her. "We all grew up on the same street. Except for Stephen. He didn't move to our street until we were in grade four. He's the newcomer."

Ellen can't remember a single person from her grade four class. She didn't remember going to kindergarten. Her first clear memory of school was from grade eight, when a girl who sat near her skipped a grade. Ellen remembered her only because everyone said she was teacher's pet and that's why she skipped.

Even high school was a blur. She remembered about ten names. Four of them were people everyone knew, the "in" group — the first to wear the latest fad to school, the first to streak their hair in colours, the first to carry their books in backpacks.

She had known who they were, but they didn't know her. They said hi when they passed in the hall, but they said hi to everyone. Ellen had desperately wanted to be one of them, but didn't know how.

"Hey, look! Ellen's got her sweater on backward," Lloyd chortled.

Her mother glanced across the kitchen and smiled.

"Doesn't it hurt to sit against the buttons like that?" Lloyd asked.

"Is it so no one can tell if you're coming or going?" her father teased.

"This is the new way to wear cardigans," Ellen had explained. "It's the latest style."

A few months later, there was another fashion "must have" — an angora collar.

"Please, Mom," she begged. "Everyone has one. I'll never ask for anything else, but I really, really want an angora collar."

"They're too expensive," her mother replied.

Ellen knew that she could buy a pair of shoes for the price of the collar, but she didn't care. She wanted one like she'd never wanted anything in her whole life.

A few days later, her mother had a surprise for her. She'd made a fur collar. Ellen recognized the fur. It had been trimmed from her mother's old coat.

Ellen took the collar in her hands, fighting to hold back tears. She didn't know what to do with it. It wasn't angora. It was the wrong colour. It was cut wrong. It was wrong, wrong, wrong.

"Thanks, Mom," she said, trying to breathe normally. "That's wonderful."

She put it in her drawer. She never wore it.

Soon after, the "in" group wore something else. It didn't matter. Ellen never made it into their group. She never made it into any group.

Ellen joined the High School Annual Society, because they were always short of help. She joined the band. There was no place for her violin, but the band master handed her a trumpet. After school, when the popular kids turned out for team sports — track and field, cheerleading — or just hung out together, she had an excuse for not joining them.

"Sorry, I've got band practice," she would say.

Even when there was no practice, she would stay and work on the trumpet by herself. It was an ugly instrument that left her lips red and swollen and her cheeks aching, and filled her mouth with the taste of brass. Still, she stayed with it during the year she spent at that school.

She fast forwards to graduation. She and Al got married. Within a few years, most of his buddies were married, too. The couples saw each other socially once in a while, but Ellen wasn't included in the "wives group" that met for lunch, or shopping, or to swap babysitting when someone had a hairdresser's appointment.

Once, they asked her to join them.

"Al, the girls are going to the Craft Fair on Saturday and they've asked me to go with them. I could maybe get a few things for Christmas."

He had looked at her blankly.

"This Saturday?"

Something in his voice turned off her enthusiasm.

"Why — are we doing something this Saturday?"

He shook his head sadly.

"No. Not really. It's just that Saturday is about the only day we have together. I look forward to our Saturdays."

"It won't be all day," she protested.

The silence curdled around her. Then he smiled, a small, sad smile.

"I know. It's just that our time together is so special. I'm being selfish. You go ahead and have a good time. I'll stay here with the kids. Maybe we can do something together next Saturday."

It sounded romantic. He loved her so much he couldn't bear to give up any of their precious time together. How could she resist? She phoned back and made her regrets.

"I'm sorry. I forgot about something we'd planned for Saturday," she said.

"That's okay. We'll get together another time."

But they never do.

That particular Saturday, Al spent most of the morning at the building supply store getting sheets of plastic to put over the basement windows. Once he'd bought the plastic, it seemed silly not to put it up while the weather was still dry and he could work outdoors.

"It'll be a lot warmer downstairs," he told her. "There's lots of room to fix up a playroom for the kids. And I'd like to put in a workshop. I really need a place for all my tools and stuff."

She stayed upstairs, doing something or other. They would have spent the same amount of time together if she'd gone to the craft fair. The other couples they knew spent a lot of time together, going off in fours and sixes and even spending summer holidays together. They went in large groups to the lake where they rented adjoining cabins. Ellen and Al were never included.

Ellen wondered if it was her fault. Had she missed some signals somewhere? Had she forgotten to make the proper response? Was there some kind of pheromone she lacked, pheromones that everyone else had?

She couldn't fault Al. He worked all week. He was increasingly busy in the evenings and on weekends. What with his sports teams and his meetings, he didn't have much free time. And as he said, you couldn't join a team or promise to serve on a committee and not show up. Ellen made sure dinner was ready as soon as he came home from work so he wouldn't be late for whatever he was doing that evening.

When he didn't have to go out, he spent time downstairs, working on the playroom, or in his workshop. Ellen wasn't exactly sure what he did down there. He ate dinner, watched the news, and then disappeared downstairs. She didn't see him again until the late night news came on, just before bedtime.

At times she heard him on the telephone, but she was never sure who he was talking to and she was afraid to ask. She only did it once.

"Who was that?"

"Just a fellow I know."

"What did he want?"

"What is this, an inquisition? He wanted to talk to me, that's all. If it concerned you, I'd tell you."

Ellen held back her tears. She was being childish. He was right. She didn't need to know about every little thing he did, or everyone he talked to.

Once in a while they would go to a Saturday night party at one of his friends' homes. At intervals they would have a party at their home, when they were overdue for social payback. But the intervals grew longer and longer and she discovered that, while the Saturday night parties continued, they were no longer on the guest list.

They were drifting away. She wasn't sure where, or what to do about it.

One night, when the kids were all in school, Al volunteered to stay home and babysit so Ellen could go to parent-teacher night.

"It'll do you good to get out," he told her.

"We could get a sitter so you can come, too," she protested.

"No, that's all right. I don't mind staying home with the kids."

"Don't you want to meet their teachers?"

"You can do it. You know more about that sort of thing. Anyway, it's hard to get a sitter on a school night."

"It's not *that* hard," she countered. "We won't be staying out late. The interviews are all over by 8:30 or 9:00 at the latest."

Al nodded. "Yeah, but by the time we go somewhere for a snack afterward, it's getting pretty late."

"We can come home for a snack."

Al shrugged. "No, it's okay. You go. I'll stay with the kids."

Dutifully she went to the parent-teacher meetings and brought home vague reports on the kids' progress. They got passing grades but she was sure they could do better. Was it her fault? Al's fault? The teacher's fault? She couldn't put her finger on what was wrong. She hated to talk to anyone about it. It seemed disloyal to the kids, and to Al.

The pattern built over the years. Now, when she needs a friend, there is literally no one she can call.

✳

"How are you supposed to make friends anyway?" she asks herself, crossly. Taking armloads of books from the library isn't very effective. The only people Ellen sees are the librarians, who know her name only because it's on her library card; but she doesn't know their names and has never thought to ask.

She could maybe join a church group, but there's a lot of baggage on that route and Ellen isn't sure she could handle it right now. She's beginning to understand why people join singles clubs. Meeting people and making friends isn't as easy as everyone assumes. As a joke, she makes up her own classified ad: married woman, non-smoker, seeking ... Ellen can't think of anything to put in. She doesn't know what to ask for. She doesn't know who she's looking for. There's a tremendous vacuum in her life, but she doesn't know what to fill it with.

Do other people feel this way, too?

She thinks back to the day she got her bike. The young man at the mall told her to join a bike club.

"It's more fun with other people," he said.

She's sure he was right, but she doesn't know where the bike clubs are or how to reach them. She looks in the phone book, but there's nothing listed in the yellow pages. She doesn't know where else to look.

Ellen watches bikers along the highway. They're usually men, very lean, and they travel in packs, like foraging wolves — heads down, teeth clenched, butts tight. Not about to accept a soft, undertrained female into the group. There must be some women out there, or other beginners.

Everyone has to start somewhere, she tells herself, *even bikers.*

What she needs is a group of neophytes, preferably pudgy, out-of-shape neophytes. It doesn't matter if they're male or female, just that she can keep up with them.

There's a sport association office near the mall. She's passed it hundreds of times. Surely they know about bike clubs? Ellen phones one day, before she can talk herself out of it. It seems to be a good starting point. The voice on the phone tells her there are dozens of bike clubs, ranging from the heavy duty racers to long-distance riders who go across North America. These are offered as opposite ends of a scale, but the entire scale is beyond her reach.

In desperation, she calls both groups. Both encourage her to turn out for a session with them.

"But I'm not a racer," she tells the race group.

"No problem," a cheerful young woman replies. "We weren't racers when we started either. We go on lots of training runs and you'd probably enjoy that. When the competitions are on, the rest of us help out with timing, scorekeeping, marshalling, and that sort of thing."

Ellen jots down some times and dates and promises she'll think about it.

The long-distance riders invite her to come for a session with them.

"I can't go very far," she tells them.

"No problem," an older man replies. "We couldn't either, when we first began."

Why does she feel she's already had this conversation? He assures her she can ride along with the group on their training runs. And she'll be welcomed as a helper on the serious rides — keeping track of times and distances, helping out on the SAG wagon.

Now she knows she's had this conversation before.

"You'll be going the distance before you know it," he concludes cheerfully.

Once again, she jots down dates and times and promises to think about it.

＊

The next day Ellen finds a riding group by accident when she's biking home from the post office. Five women wheel into the little park next door and begin stretching. She pedals over and watches them for a moment.

"Hi. Come join us," one offers.

The others laugh. "Right. There's enough agony for all."

Intrigued, Ellen dismounts, parks her bike, and asks the name of the group.

"We're the Middle of the Road Gang. Too young to be seniors, too old to be racers, so we ride just for the fun of it."

"Where do you go?"

"Different places. Generally we do a loop somewhere. Last year we went to Victoria. Our husbands dropped us off at the ferry and we biked into Victoria. It was a great trip!"

Smiles and laughter affirm her statement. Ellen is suitably impressed.

The woman continues. "Our goal this year is to do Vashon Island. You can take the ferry from Seattle to one end and catch the ferry to Tacoma at the other end. We want to stay on the island for a couple of days. It's hard for some of us to get away for longer than that."

One of the other women adds, "Even if we never do it, we can dream about it."

A flood of comments swirls around her statement, ripples in the flow of conversation, followed by a spatter of introductions.

"You're welcome to ride with us," Penny adds. She's a smiling blonde who looks like Ellen has always wanted to look — pert, perky, and pretty.

"We're working on conditioning," she adds. "We do a couple of short sessions during the week. It makes the weekend trip easier."

"Do you always meet here?" Ellen asks.

"No. We just came to get a yogurt cone."

One of the women laughs. "Yogurt's healthy."

"Sure. It doesn't have any calories either," another adds.

"Why don't you join us?"

The moment teeters.

"We aren't going far."

The pattern kicks in again. Ellen automatically starts to say no. There are things she has to do. Then she stops. There is nothing she has to do. No one cares if she comes home in an hour, or a week — or ever, for that matter.

"Sure," she says. "But I'll pass on the yogurt."

"We've already done that," Susan says. She's the one with the long ponytail hanging down from her helmet

Penny agrees: "It's a reward for good behaviour."

"Right," Megan adds. "We celebrate burning off all those calories by taking on a whole new load of calories."

There is a general hooting at this.

None is chubby, fat, or overweight. Two are big boned in a way that looks healthy, but not like they have a weight problem. Ellen is surprised that they even care about calories or weight loss.

"We're heading down the highway today," Susan says. "There are some nice roller coaster rides just a few miles along."

"Yeah." Megan smiles. "If we do really good on the roller coaster, we treat ourselves to carrot cake at the tea room."

"Yum, yum," Penny enthuses. "Carrot cake. Everyone knows how healthy that is. Just like yogurt. I might even have two."

"Only if you pedal up the roller coaster backward," Susan decrees.

Laughter again.

This begins to make sense. They're making fun of themselves. No, Ellen corrects herself, they aren't making fun of themselves. They're making fun of women as stereotypes, or the notion that this is the way women behave.

Ellen wants very much to be part of this group. She wants to know them. She wants to spend time with them. She wants to be friends with them.

They push off, forming a single line in the right-hand lane.

Susan takes the lead, Megan goes second. Penny, the lean blonde, goes third, followed by Patty. Patty has bright fluorescent bike pants and wears a matching helmet cover.

"Visibility is my middle name," she says, smiling, when Ellen comments on her outfit. "Anyway, I make them myself, so I can go a little crazy."

Megan slots Ellen into the lineup between herself and Penny.

"It's easier to put new people in the middle of the group," she explains. "We're used to riding together and checking to make sure no one straggles or has problems."

There is constant chatter among the women, with comments passed up and down the line.

"Look out ahead," Susan warns. "There's some stuff on the road."

"Loose gravel coming up," Penny cautions.

"Extra-wide load behind," Megan calls out. "Keep as far right as you can."

They cross a bridge, strung out in a neat line. The lanes seem very narrow here, but widen again once they pass the bridge, with a good shoulder lane. It's comfortable riding.

Ellen feels warm now. Susan is setting a good pace. It's a little faster than she's accustomed to, but she can keep up. She feels it in her legs and, surprisingly, in her shoulders.

"There's a little shopping plaza ahead, with the Golden Arches on the corner."

"Time for a water break," Patty announces.

Susan leads the line in, then turns to Ellen as they park their bikes.

"How's it going? Is the pace okay for you?"

"Perfect."

Susan laughs. She has a wonderful laugh, warm, friendly, and genuine.

"The next part is easy. There's a bit of a hill going up — nothing that will give you any trouble — then a long, swooping downhill. We stay right over on that one. It starts as two lanes at the top of the hill, but converges into one, so there's sometimes cars juggling for space in line. We'll take it easy."

"What comes after that?"

"We head over to the ferry."

Ellen is puzzled.

"It's a little free ferry," Susan explains. "It goes back and forth more or less on demand. There's lots of good riding on the other side. The roads don't have much of a shoulder, but there isn't much traffic either."

They set off again. Susan is right. The uphill is no problem and the long coast down is pure pleasure. Ellen stands on her pedals as they cross a set of train tracks, then turn down a side road paste a cedar mill. The saw buzzes and whines its way through a log, sending an invisible current of scent through the air, a scent that reminds Ellen of her mom's cedar doily box. A few minutes later, they're at the ferry loading zone, where an attendant waves them through.

"Walk your bikes on," she reminds them.

They go ahead of the automobiles, moving with a couple of pedestrians. At the front of the ferry there's a blocked-off area bounded by yellow painted pipes, where bikes can stand out of the way of traffic. The women prop the bikes on kickstands and themselves on the wide, breast-high rail, looking out over the river.

The far shore shows sedentary rows of people. Along the edge of the water there's a row of deck chairs and people fishing. Farther back, clusters of people sit or stand in little groups. A couple of picnics happen on tailgates of trucks in the parking lot.

Little kids crouch down, digging trenches and building whatever it is kids build in the sand. Bigger kids run around, making mechanical noises while their parents ignore them.

The ferry noses into its slip, unloads one group of passengers and loads another and chugs back to the other side.

The women leave the ferry and push their bikes up a metal ramp. There's a splintery wood sidewalk at the top of the ramp that keeps pedestrians and bikes out of the traffic. The cars have a wooden road, too. It hasn't been there long enough to begin disintegrating, but it's old enough to have weathered to a silvery base. Twin ribbons of black, reminders of thousands of tires, draw a line from the ferry ramp to the waiting highway. Ellen listens as the cars rumble pleasantly along. A loose board creates a mambo of thumps as the cars drive past.

At the far end of the ramp there's a washroom that draws the group like tacks to a magnet; facilities are hard to come by for bikers.

As the ride progresses, Ellen feels more and more constricted. She wants to keep going. She doesn't want to stop and wait for everyone else. She doesn't want to stop and look around. She doesn't want to comment on everything she sees. These are nice people, friendly and open. Another time, another place, and she'd be happy to be part of their group, but what she wants now is to be at one with the road, not be interrupted by the never-ending ripple of chatter that accompanies them.

Later that afternoon, when they near Ellen's apartment block, she peels away quietly and heads for home while the rest carry on, chirping like a flock of multicoloured sparrows. She changes gears and speeds away, pumping as fast as she can until the blood pounds in her ears and her breath strains and burns against her chest.

That was bad of me, she acknowledges to herself, *but I couldn't think of another way to escape.*

Flushed and happy, she pulls into her driveway just as one of the others residents is leaving the building. He smiles, holds the door, and motions her in.

"Good ride?" he asks.

"Great," she affirms. Her eyes flick rapidly over him. Hard to define his age — somewhere around hers, but maybe a few years younger. There's a flutter of grey over his temples.

"I've seen you go out before." He smiles. "I ride too. It's a great neighbourhood for that, isn't it?"

That explains the lean, fit look of him and the suntan that sets off his deep blue eyes. Sooty eyes, her father used to call them. Celtic eyes.

She nods, pushing her bike into the lobby as he releases the door and gives her a cheerful wave.

"Have a good day," he says, as the door whooshes shut behind him.

An hour later she's surprised by a knock on her door. When she opens it, it's the same man.

"You should have put the chain on first," he scolds. "Not a good idea to open the door before you know who's there, so I'll introduce myself. I'm Tim, your neighbour two doors down the hall."

"Ellen," she replies, holding out her hand.

He shakes her hand, then stretches his other hand forward.

"There. You dropped this when you came in."

Her bike glove.

"Thank you. I didn't realize I'd lost it."

As he smiles, she's struck by a sudden question.

"How did you know where I lived?"

"That's easy. I followed your tracks down the hall."

"My tracks?"

Laughing, he pulls her arm gently, leading her into the hall.

"There. Over on the side. See the marks on the carpet from your tires? It doesn't take a genius to follow them to your apartment.

"Now in you go, back home again. And next time, put the chain on the door before you open it. Even for me."

Smiling, he repeats his cheery salute. She watches, bemused, as he walks two doors down the hall to enter his own apartment.

— 7 —

THE SOAP BOTTLE BLOWS a raspberry, spraying clusters of tiny bubbles onto the dishwater. A miniscule bulge of liquid sags from the end of the spout, swaying over the dirty dishes, then retreats back into the bottle. Ellen shakes it crossly, trying to squeeze out a few more drops. Her eyes flick to the slip of paper pinned to the fridge by a pair of magnetic pigs. What was once a short, orderly list is now jammed with scribbled reminders of things she needs.

In those long-ago days before her life changed, she spent entire afternoons shopping. Now she shops only when she has to. Money is getting tight and she's afraid to spend it. She doesn't want to see things she wants. She doesn't like to see things she likes. She buys what she has to, but only that.

She unscrews the bottle cap, runs a little water inside and swishes it around to pick up the last traces of detergent before pouring it into the sink. Carefully, she caps the empty bottle and puts it aside for recycling before blotting her hands on the dish towel, grabbing a pencil, and adding dish detergent to her list. A missed droplet of water trickles down the underside of her wrist as she writes.

In a moment of whimsy, she remembers last night's decision and adds another word to the list: *CALIFORNIA*. She prints it in big block letters, steps back to look, and smiles.

She's going to California.

She's going to California on her bike.

She's going to California on her bike, by herself.

Ellen repeats the words in her mind, like a magic mantra, then realizes there's no one to overhear her. She can say it out loud. She does, first whispering, then speaking, and finally shouting: "I'm going to California on my bike, all by myself!"

The sound rumbles through her throat and echoes in her chest. She likes the way the words feel, filling her mouth and tumbling from her lips. She half expects them to hang in the air, like words in a comic strip balloon. She's surprised by her bravado. She's never shouted out loud for no reason at all, not caring whether anyone hears her or not. So many things, she thinks, so many things she's never done. Never been to Disneyland, never been to Universal Studios, or Knott's Berry Farm. Never strolled on Sunset Boulevard or watched for stars on Rodeo Drive. Never been to Muscle Beach or seen bronzed and handsome surfers ride their boards on the curling waves off Ventura. But she's heard the names and seen pictures in magazines, movies, and on television until they've become familiar in her mind, like the "old country" her father talked about in his stories until they became part of her memories.

There are a thousand places she's never been. Someday she'll go to New York City, walk down Broadway, look up at the sky-scrapers, and wander in Central Park. Someday she'll go to Paris and see the Eiffel Tower. Someday she'll visit a tropical island. But first, she's going to California.

She's happy with her choice. Anyone can fly, or go by train, or bus, even drive. All that takes is money. She doesn't want to be a conventional tourist. It's too ordinary and too easy. This has to be something special, something memorable, something unique. If she were younger and it was thirty years ago, when life was gentler, she might hitch-hike, but hundreds of people have done that, so it's no longer anything special. And from a purely practical point of view, it's no longer safe. Going by bike is different. There's something slightly wacky about it, something eccentric, and something deliciously scary in going alone. One is as important as the other. All her life Ellen has done only the things that other people do, and done them the way that other people do them. The expected things. The nice things. The safe things.

All her life she's been afraid: Afraid of the dark. Afraid of being alone. Afraid of strangers. Afraid of men. Afraid to walk down a dark street at night. Afraid to run down a wooded jogging trail. Afraid of too many things. She needs this trip to prove to herself that she has nothing to be afraid of anymore. That's not quite true. There are still things to be afraid of, but those are legitimate things, not nameless spectres. She can be cautious, yes, responsible, of course. But she rejects the notion of fear for no reason at all.

California. It's a wonderful word. It leaves a special taste in her mouth when she says it — a golden brown, sweet, nutty taste, like the hint of chocolate across her tongue.

Ellen wishes there was someone who could share the news and be excited with her. The kids would probably try to talk her out of it, so she'll tell them later. She might not say anything at all — just phone when she gets there. Briefly, she considers telling Al, but if he knew she was planning any sort of a trip he'd decide she was getting too much money and find a way to make her give some of it back. But it doesn't matter that there's no one to share the news. She encloses the glow inside her, so she can touch it gently during the day. At that moment, her doorbell rings.

Startled, she opens the door a crack.

"Hi there. It's Tim. I've got something for you."

She swings the door open and steps into the hall.

"I've watched you go through the front door with your bike — you must have the patience of a saint to do that every time you go in or out. Here. Stick this in your pocket."

He proffers a small, inch-thick plastic wedge.

"Jam it under the door and it will keep the door open while you go through. Just remember to pick it up after," he explains. "Oh — and you can keep your bike in one piece in the elevator if you stand it up on the back wheel."

As she stammers her thanks, he peeks over her shoulder into the apartment and spots the piled up cardboard boxes.

"You aren't moving, are you?"

"Oh, no. Well ... actually, I haven't really unpacked. I haven't decided where to put everything yet."

"Ah. Well. If you're needing help, feel free to ask."

"I'll do that. Thank you."

He steps away slowly, then turns back.

"I usually have a morning cuppa about this time. I'd enjoy a little company."

Her first impulse is to refuse. Then her California bravado takes over.

"I'd like that."

He nods, smiling. "Right. Give me a minute to get the kettle boiling. You know where I am, don't you? Second apartment down the hall, on your left."

"I'll be there in a few minutes. And thank you. Thank you for the door stopper."

Stupid! She rages at herself. How could she have been so stupid? Door stoppers weren't invented a week ago. She had door stoppers in her house, for heaven's sake. Why did she never think to go to the hardware store and buy one? What a comic figure she must have looked. How many other people laughed at her?

She tidies her hair and puts on a clean sweatshirt before walking down the hall. Maybe she can make a new friend after all.

She's startled by his apartment. Place of honour is occupied by an easel, and swatches of fabric are pinned to the walls, interspersed with watercolour sketches.

He laughs as he follows her gaze.

"I'm designing a set."

She has no idea what he's talking about.

"For a stage play. That's what I do, I design sets — the backgrounds — for plays."

Their conversation is friendly, but the tea is good. She learns a little about him. He's not married, but along with his set designs, he's involved with weddings.

"I probably go to a couple of weddings every week," he announces, then laughs. "I'm a freelance wedding photographer, as well — sort of an odd-job specialist. Actually, I was wondering if you do anything on Saturdays."

Her eyes snap wide in shock. A date? It's been forever since she dated anyone. Then he laughs.

"No, not what you're thinking. I've got a wedding scheduled in a couple of weeks — on a Saturday, when most weddings seem to be — and I could use a little help, if you're free." He pauses. "Weddings today are a lot more interesting than they used to be."

He regales her with stories about weddings on mountain tops. "Easy for the bride and groom. I'll never forget the first one I did. They — and the rest of the wedding party except for the parents — were all members of a hiking club, so they just sprinted up the mountain. Mom and Dad staggered along after. The JP had a really hard go of it. He was pretty much out of shape and I thought we were going to have to prop him up to do the vows."

"And you?"

"I had to carry all my camera gear up the mountain — reflectors, film bag, tripod, all that sort of stuff. Nearly killed me! That's when I started to think about hiring an assistant for some of my shoots. I can't afford to hire someone full time or even regular part time, because the jobs aren't on any regular schedule. But if you'd like to come once in a while, I could pay you something for your time.

"But I don't know anything about photography."

"No problem. The helper doesn't have anything to do with the cameras, and I probably wouldn't need you for all the weddings. It could be convenient for us both, what with you living just down the hall. You wouldn't even have to drive — I'd provide taxi service."

He leaves the table and rummages on a desktop.

"Here — this is what I'm talking about."

He plops an envelope on the table. "Go ahead. Open it."

Carefully she extracts a wedding invitation.

"We're taking the plunge," it announces. Below that is a picture of two people wearing wetsuits, fins, masks, and snorkels. They could be a couple, two men, two women — or two Martians. The inside page invites family and friends to join the happy couple on the dock at Rocky Point where they'll board a dive boat, head for a special spot, and the couple will be married.

Divers were invited to join in an underwater reception, to be followed by a dry land reception at the Paradigm Hall.

She looks at him blankly.

"I can't dive."

"No matter. You don't have to. I'm certified. What I hoped you might do is help me on the boat, arranging shots, holding the remote flash — same sort of thing that you'd do on dry land at the reception. I can handle the underwater pictures by myself."

She smiles weakly. She hates boats, doesn't know anything about photography or diving, and doesn't know anything about this person. She doesn't want to go, but is unsure how to get out of it.

"Come on — give it a try. What have you got to lose?"

He takes her silence for consent.

"Good for you. I'll make the arrangements and we can go in my car. It's still a couple of weeks away, so there's no panic. I can show you the equipment one evening before then, so you'll know how to handle it."

Numbly, she nods before rising to her feet.

"I guess I'd better be getting back now. Thank you for the tea."

Cheerily, he picks up the tea cups and sees her to the door, then watches until she enters her own apartment.

Once inside, she vents her anger on a pillow, pounding it with her fists. "You ninny! You absolute spineless nit."

As she rages around the apartment, she trips against one of the piled-up boxes, falling clumsily to the floor, twisting her ankle as she lands. A stab of pain jolts through her, taking the breath from her lungs. "Please," she prays. "Please don't let it be broken."

In a few minutes the pain diminishes enough that she can struggle awkwardly to her feet. It might not be broken, but it certainly isn't working very well. Maybe a sprain, or maybe she just twisted it. In any case, ice cubes will help. She hobbles to the fridge and pours ice into a plastic bag, packs it around her ankle, and wraps it in place with a towel.

So much for the independent lady who was going to California, the one who wasn't going to let people impose on her ever again, the one who was going to be strong and forthright.

※

The next morning Ellen's ankle is still tender but once again usable. She resists an impulse to kick the offending box and strips it open instead, digging out the contents and finding places to store them. When it's empty, she attacks the next box. By midday, the long-ignored boxes have been opened, emptied, and stacked neatly by the door, ready to go to the recycling bin in the back alley.

Maybe there's hope for her after all. And maybe California isn't that impossible either. Still, there are practical things she has to do first. One is to get a good map, figure out where her stopping points will be, and make a list of motels along the way.

For the first time since the divorce, Ellen feels like a whole person. It's more than independence, it's being hugely non-dependent. She doesn't need to depend on anyone, and no one depends on her for anything. No husband, no child, not even a cat. That brings a light-headed sense of freedom. It's like being a child again, only better. She doesn't have to ask permission anymore. She's surprised to find herself humming. She doesn't even know the tune, but it's a happy little song that matches her mood.

She glances at her left hand — the wedding ring is no longer bracketed by bulges. *Have I really lost that much weight?* she asks herself. Her fingers twist the ring over her knuckle. It slides off quickly and easily. Curiously, she examines it, looking inside. It would have been romantic to engrave their initials inside, or their wedding date, but Al hadn't done either.

What now? she wonders. Surely nothing is more useless than a used wedding ring. She can't wear it, she can't give it away — no one wants a used wedding ring. She remembers a day long ago when she stood on the beach at English Bay watching the annual Polar Bear Swim on New Year's Day. Hundreds of hardy, or hung-over swimmers turned out for the annual event, which was watched by hundreds more, dressed warmly against the cold winter wind. Lifeguards patrolled the water in rowboats.

On that particular day, a woman had detached herself from the onlookers and followed the swimmers in their lemming-like rush to the water.

"There you go, you bastard. She can have it — I don't want it. Or you, either," she yelled.

With that, she'd flung something gold and glittering into the water, then turned, tears coursing down her cheeks, as she ran back up the beach.

Ellen laughs at herself. It's too late to offer sympathy, but at least she understands now what the woman was doing.

Her mind reverts to her current goal.

There's an automobile association office near the mall. They should have what she needs to figure out a route.

"No time like the present," she tells herself, then laughs. It's her mother's voice she hears. Ellen heard those words a million times in her teens. Her mom believed there was no time like the present for getting things done. Unpleasant things, jobs she didn't want to do, difficult chores, uncompleted homework, extra practise on the violin — whatever led her to procrastination would be over the sooner for getting at it right away. And the things she wanted to do ... well, there was no time like the present for doing something enjoyable!

Ellen almost feels her mom standing just out of sight. If she turns her head quickly and looks hard, she'll see her, just around the corner.

"We didn't always see eye to eye," Ellen tells her, "but as I get older, I understand you better." Somehow, she's sure her mom hears her. She wonders what her mother would have been like had she reached this age, had she not been killed in the crash. Had she gone on to develop her own life, her own thoughts, her own ideas, without being eternally squashed under her husband's thumb. A feeling of kinship with her mother has replaced the anger and resentment she once felt.

She pops the panniers on her bike, buckles on her fanny pack, and wheels into the hall. Just as she reaches the lobby, the letter carrier enters, pulling a handful of mail from her canvas carry bag and swinging open the large door that covers the pigeonhole boxes. She sorts letters quickly and efficiently into the various slots that stand, blank and empty, like the gaping mouths of baby birds, waiting to be fed.

Ellen peeks over her shoulder as a fat envelope lands in her box.

"Oh! That's mine!"

The carrier turns and smiles. "Got any ID?"

Ellen unzips her fanny pack and fishes out her wallet, flipping it open to show her driver's licence. The carrier looks at it briefly, comparing Ellen to the picture on the card.

"Okay. Here you go." She removes the envelope from Ellen's box and passes it to her.

Ellen laughs at herself as she thanks the carrier and wriggles her way through the door. It could have waited until she came back, but there's something irresistibly urgent about a freshly delivered letter.

She glances at the handwriting. It's from her daughter Joanne. Quickly she nudges the kickstand in place and rips open the envelope. It begins with the usual stuff — there's some artwork enclosed to replace older pictures on her fridge door. Then, near the bottom of the letter, comes the meat of the message. It's typical of Joanne to edge into what she really wants to say.

Mom — I've tried phoning but I never seem to catch you in. I know you don't like answering machines, but there are times when they are useful. I need to talk to you. Can you phone me as soon as you get this? Please. You should get this Tuesday afternoon, so please call me Tuesday evening or Wednesday morning. Thanks.

Love you.

A scrawled *J* drifts off into a series of loops that probably spelled out Joanne once upon a time, but now just carve a trail across the paper.

Ellen debates whether to go to the store and the library first or go back upstairs and phone right away. Logically, she should get her errands done, since she's out already, but logic doesn't swing much weight when it flies against maternal emotions.

She slides the letter back into its envelope and tucks it in her fanny pack, then fishes out her key. Minutes later, Joanne's phone is ringing. She must have been close by. She answers on the third ring.

"It's me, dear," Ellen says. "I just got your letter. What's wrong?"

There's a micro-second pause before Joanne answers.

"I didn't want to upset you."

"But something is wrong," Ellen persists. "Don't dance around it — just go ahead and tell me."

That was another of her mother's sayings. Don't dance around it. Spit it out.

"Okay, Mom. No dancing. Lissy has a problem. We didn't know anything was wrong — I mean, she never complained or anything and everything seemed normal."

Her voice starts to climb, rising to a question mark, just as it did when she was a little girl.

Ellen interrupts. "Joanne, just tell me."

There's a pause while Joanne takes a breath. Ellen pictures her rubbing her forehead with her fingers as she searches for words.

"Lissy has some kind of tumour and it's bad. They did some tests yesterday and they operate this week."

Her voice stops for a moment. Ellen can hear her breathing, very controlled, as though she's trying hard not to cry. She's always been that way. If Jennifer got stung by a bee, she'd holler bloody murder, but not Joanne. The more she hurt, the quieter she got. Ellen tries to think of something to say that isn't soppy. Before she finds the words, Joanne continues.

"Mom, she's too little for this. It shouldn't be happening. Please, could you come for a while? Maybe spend some time with Jana while we're at the hospital with Lissy?"

Ellen's stomach turns cold. She has sudden queasy thoughts about what they might be dealing with.

"Joanne ... what kind of tumour is it?"

The phone buzzes in her ear, sickening waves ride along the wires. She knows, even before Joanne replies.

"It's the bad one, Mom. Cancer. It's growing fast and it's vicious in little kids. There's a chance if they get it early, but they usually find it by accident because there aren't many symptoms.

The doctor gave us some stuff to read, but it's just so much gibberish right now. All I know is she's sick. Really sick."

There's a pause.

"Mom … can you come?"

"You know I'll be there. Don't even think about it."

"Thanks, Mom. That helps a lot. Look, I don't want to talk about this on the phone. Every time I think about it I get all upset and start crying and that doesn't help anything. We don't want to say too much in front of Jana. Stan and I have been playing it cool so she doesn't get too upset."

"When's the surgery scheduled?"

"Thursday," Joanne whispers. "I know it's awfully short notice, but—"

Ellen interrupts. "It's not a problem. Today's Tuesday. Let me make a reservation. I'll call you back as soon as I have something confirmed."

"Thanks, Mom."

Ellen hears tears creeping into her voice.

"Now don't you start crying. Not on long distance. Too expensive. Save your tears for when I get there. It's much cheaper that way. And besides, I can give you a hug."

Joanne starts to laugh. "Thanks, Mom."

They go through quick goodbyes and hang up.

Ellen flips open the phone book and starts calling airlines, trying to find the impossible combination of an immediate opening and a low fare. She rummages in her purse for something to write on and pulls out her shopping list.

CALIFORNIA laughs back at her from the page. The golden honey has turned to grit. She listens carefully to one airline agent and writes down dates, times, flights, and fares. She's shocked at the cost. She calls another airline. The prices are about the same.

"I didn't realize it was going to be so expensive," Ellen says. "I'm sure the prices in the travel ads were about half that much."

"The low rates have to be paid at least two weeks in advance of the flight — and a month for the really low ones," the agent replies.

"Two weeks or a month ago, I didn't know I'd have to go."

There is a moment of silence. "Is this an emergency? If it's compassionate, there are special fares for that. I mean, if there's a death in the family, we do give a discount."

Ellen shakes her head, then realizes the agent can't see her. It isn't a death in the family. There isn't going to *be* a death in the family. It's a simple operation. Ellen's afraid to tempt fate by telling her why she has to go.

"It isn't a death," she blurts out. "My granddaughter is going in for surgery."

"I'm sorry, but that doesn't qualify," the agent replies.

Ellen makes a reservation and calls Joanne back to tell her she'll arrive Wednesday at noon.

"Thanks, Mom. Someone will be there to meet you."

"Don't worry about it," Ellen says quickly. "I'll just take a cab to the house and see you there."

She pulls out a suitcase and tries to order her thoughts. What to take? The weather is still pleasant so she won't need a heavy coat. Sweats are fine for daytime — comfortable and easy. Slacks and a blouse in case she has to go anywhere dressier than sweats. A medium sweater. It might be cool in the evening. A pair of fleecy pyjamas. The PJs are heavy enough that she won't need a dressing gown. As an afterthought she throws in a couple of T-shirts, a pair of shorts, and a bathing suit. She can't take her bike, but maybe she can find an hour for herself at the rec centre near Joanne's house. There's an indoor running track and a pretty good pool. It might be a good place to take Jana, too. She's going to need some special attention, no matter what happens.

Ellen finishes packing. Her cosmetic case, which doesn't hold much in the line of cosmetics, but keeps her toothbrush, toothpaste, and vitamins together, tucks into the corner of her bag.

Restlessly, she tidies up the apartment. Clean sheets on the bed so it will be ready for her when she gets back. Empty the fridge of leftovers and bits and pieces of stuff that might not keep. There isn't much. One person doesn't generate many leftovers. All her plants are artificial — lovely, but not real. One of her neighbours used to laugh at her fondness for fake flowers.

"All I can smell in your house is silk," she would tease. That's true, but no one has to water silk. Silk flowers don't droop and die if someone forgets about them, nor do they breed colonies of weird little bugs that scurry out of sight whenever a leaf is turned. And they don't need re-potting. Ellen loves real flowers, but they belong outside in a real garden where she can enjoy working with them. She hates being cooped up indoors, and she's sure flowers do, too.

She cancels the newspaper and takes her books back to the library. Then there's nothing else to do. It seems strange that getting ready is so easy now. Anytime she and Al went on vacation there were endless lists of things she had to do and they always ended up squabbling about something. She can't remember why. Nor does she remember why the travel itself seemed so complicated. Maybe it's because she only has to worry about tidying up her own life now, not fending for five other people as well.

✳

On Wednesday morning, she locks the apartment and leaves, catching an early bus. Traffic is as bad as ever and the drive to the airport is endless. She's given herself lots of extra time and that was a good thing, because she needs it all.

"You don't have much time," the agent warns as she tags Ellen's bag. "You have to go directly to the boarding gate."

Ellen sprints for the departure lounge, where boarding is already in progress. Cabin attendants rush her to her seat while they do a passenger recount. As she settles in her seat and fastens her seatbelt, she suddenly realizes that she hasn't left a message for Tim. Nor can she phone him. She doesn't know his phone number, doesn't even know his last name. Well, nothing she can do about it now. She puts the thought aside as the plane starts its lunge down the runway. This is the part of flying Ellen doesn't like. She presses her feet against the floor, tightening her butt against the seat, and wills the plane to rise. There's a small lurch, and they're airborne. Now she can relax.

The woman in the next seat has her eyes screwed shut, locking her face into a mask of denial. She, too, has bogeymen, it seems. She keeps her locked up face on during the rush down the runway, while the plane leaps into the air, and for the first few minutes of steep climbing. As the plane begins to level out, she opens her eyes, looks around, then smiles at Ellen. She takes off her glasses and focuses on them as she carefully cleans each lens.

"I always wonder if we're really going to make it," she says in such a low voice Ellen can hardly hear her. Is she whispering to herself or is she initiating conversation? Ellen doesn't want to talk to anyone right now. There are too many things to think about. She pretends she doesn't hear the woman and makes a great show of yawning, rubbing the flat little portion of her ears above the lobes, and very visibly working at equalizing the pressure in her ears.

A screeching pop deep within her ear signals success.

The woman watches for a moment before speaking again in that soft, whispery voice. "Does that unplug your ears? I have such a problem with that. Perhaps I should try it too."

She perches on the front of her seat, like a small bird ready to take flight at the first untoward motion.

Ellen doesn't say anything.

It doesn't matter. Ellen can tell that over the next few hours this woman will talk enough for both of them. All she needs is a warm body sitting somewhere near her and she's off. From previous trips (why does she always attract this type of seat companion?), Ellen knows that by the time the flight is over this stranger will have related her reasons for travelling, where she is going, what she will do there, what she usually does at home, and more information about herself and her family than Ellen would ever dream of sharing with a stranger.

She's right. The woman doesn't wait for an answer. She starts her monologue even as she works at evening the pressure in her ears.

"My, that does help, doesn't it? I'm surprised they don't have the girls telling us how to do that instead of all that nonsense about breathing into gas masks and blowing up life jackets."

Briefly, Ellen considers telling her those are oxygen masks, not gas masks, the attendants are women, not girls, and they inflate flotation devices, not life jackets. She reconsiders and says nothing.

"That's such a simple thing, but it certainly makes a difference, doesn't it?" the woman says, ignoring the fact that Ellen is ignoring her.

Ellen hates being rude. It's not something she does easily. That's one of her wimpy, non-assertive traits. It's less painful to put up with bores than make a statement. Maybe reading a book will send a message. She rummages through the seat pocket and pulls out the in-flight magazine. She doesn't feel like reading, but it's good camouflage. Ellen needn't have worried. The woman ignores the magazine, as though it's impossible for anything on a printed page to be more interesting than whatever is flitting around in her brain. Ellen is beginning to get annoyed.

The seatbelt light flicks off. Quickly, she unsnaps her belt and stands up. Maybe she can make it to the bathroom before the lineup starts. She's afraid to look directly at the woman, who continues her monologue. Ellen wonders how long she'll keep going before she notices no one is there to listen.

There is a short lineup already — mostly mothers with small children or babies. Ellen can't begin to imagine how they change diapers in the cramped quarters of the washroom. The line moves quickly and she's soon back in the aisle but reluctant to return to her seat. She delays by thumbing through the magazines in the special compartment on the wall next to the galley. Computing magazines, gossip magazines, fashion magazines, business magazines. Nothing catches her eye. All she really wants is a shield against her seat mate. She picks out a *People* and carries it back down the aisle.

A male cabin attendant wheels out the beverage cart as Ellen gets back to her seat.

"Beverage?" he asks. "Would you like a coffee?"

"Do you have diet soft drinks?"

He smiles. They always smile. There is a diet soft drink on the cart. No choice, though. Just Diet Coke. Not her favourite, but it'll be cold and wet. "That's fine," she tells him.

She considers trying to stop him before he fills the minuscule glass with ice cubes, then thinks better of it. The ice cubes will be cool on her tongue. And she can't talk with a mouthful of ice. Maybe she should get a bucket of it to keep her neighbour at bay.

He hands her the glass and a small foil package of pretzels.

Now her neighbour considers the options. She wants to discuss everything on the cart. No, she doesn't want a cocktail. It's much too early for beer. Coffee doesn't sit well if she has to use those powdered packets of artificial cream.

"Don't you have any real cream?" she asks, querulously.

He offers a carton of milk for her coffee.

"No, milk doesn't have enough body to it. I mean, it just dilutes the coffee, you know? And cools it, unless you heat the milk first."

The asinine discussion goes on and on until she finally settles on a glass of apple juice. Wordlessly, he passes it, along with the packet of pretzels. His eyes meet Ellen's briefly. She raises her eyebrows and his lips twitch in the smallest of smiles before he moves his cart to the next row.

Ellen sips her pop, making it last as long as possible, then begins on the ice cubes, one at a time. She focuses her attention on the magazine she doesn't really care about. In fact, she isn't sure who many of the "people" are. She's heard a few of the names but others are completely unfamiliar and she can't think why anyone should be interested in them.

Her neighbour settles back into her seat and retrieves her purse from under the seat ahead. It's a large leather purse, the size of a small briefcase. She plunks it on her lap and opens it wide, obviously searching for something. The leather is soft and worn, with the scuff marks of long service along its edges. Ellen hasn't seen a purse like that for years.

Ellen rejoices. The woman will take out a book and read quietly for a while. She watches from the corner of her eye. A *Readers Digest*-sized magazine comes out. She plunges her hand back in for something else and pulls out a pencil, peering at the point to make sure it's sharp, then flips through the pages until she comes to a half-completed crossword and sets to work.

Slowly, she runs her finger down the list of words, muttering definitions to herself and screwing up her face while she thinks about each one. Finally, something connects. She licks the end of the pencil and carefully inscribes letters inside each of the little squares. As she works, she runs her finger along the column of words, matching the across and down definitions, testing out a series of possibilities based on the letter she's just filled in. She mumbles each word as she thinks of it, chewing her lip as she ponders. First the upper lip, then the lower lip. Ellen's never seen anyone make such a production of a simple puzzle.

The woman glances at Ellen as though inviting a contribution. Ellen ignores her.

The page of Ellen's magazine blurs as the words swim together. Her mind is full of Lissy. One of the brightest and sweetest children she's ever known. She's the image of Joanne at that age, even down to the gap in her smile. Jana resembles Joanne in many ways too, but Ellen sees a lot of Stan in her, especially around the eyes. Jana is a completely different child. Lissy is quicksilver, moon dust, and butterfly wings. Jana is bread and jam and smudges on her face. Ellen loves them both dearly. She hates to play favourites, but somehow Lissy has always been special.

Ellen doesn't know much about cancer in children. She reminds herself of the strides made against leukemia. Once a death sentence, there are now effective treatments and kids do survive. Not all kids, but many of them. Maybe whatever kind Lissy has can be treated too. They've learned so much about cancer. Public support has grown. She remembers watching a television special on summer camp programs for children with cancer. She was surprised there were so many kids in treatment, and how ordinary the kids were. If you didn't know, you'd never guess they had life-threatening diseases. But it showed in little ways — their activities weren't quite as strenuous, there were lots of medical personnel around the camp, and some of the kids had an aesthetic, almost ethereal look to them, a transparency. They weren't plump and solid like other kids their age. But they weren't angels. Far from it! One of the sickest of the little boys was always pushing the behavioural envelope. Most of the kids had short haircuts — or that's how it seemed, until you realized they'd lost their hair through chemotherapy. The girls wore the same floppy hats other little girls wore. And all boys wore softball caps. Always.

Ellen has a funny vision of little boys being born with softball caps already on their heads, the visors turned neatly around to the back.

What will Lissy look like? Will she need radiation or chemo? Will she lose her hair? Change in other ways? It's hard to imagine Lissy moving at a normal pace, never mind a lethargic one. Lissy rushes headlong at life, as though she has a lifetime of living to do while everyone else is just getting started.

Ellen gives herself over to memories, replaying favourite scenes from her children's childhoods, reviewing her short list of memories of Lissy and Jana.

Eventually the captain's voice cuts through the drone of the engines as he announces the number of minutes until touchdown in Winnipeg, gives a local weather report, and thanks everyone for flying with his airline. The cabin attendants scurry up and down the aisle, picking up trash, checking trays are locked in place and seat backs are in the upright position. A woman making PA announcements reminds everyone to check for cabin baggage before deplaning. Once again the time is announced, but it's the wrong time. The voice breaks into giggles and corrects itself. Back in control, she thanks the passengers yet again for flying with them and reminds everyone that for their safety, they are to remain seated with seatbelts fastened until the plane comes to a complete halt.

✳

Stan and Jana are there to meet her.

"Gramma!" Jana yelps, launching herself at Ellen. "Gramma, you came! Lissy's in the hospital and the doctor's gonna fix her."

Ellen bends down for a hug.

"Yes, darling. I know. I thought maybe we could spend a little time together while she's getting better. Would that be a good idea?"

Jana grins. "That's a super good idea."

Ellen rises and accepts a careful hug from Stan.

"How's it going?" she asks.

He thinks for a moment before answering. "It's too soon to say." Then he turns to Jana. "Honey, could you get that cart for Grandma?" He points a few feet away where an empty baggage cart stands unclaimed.

Jana bounces off.

"Joanne's at the hospital. They started surgery about an hour ago. We won't know anything for a while yet. We're trying to keep things on an even keel so Jana doesn't get upset. It's so hard to explain at her age."

"I thought surgery was tomorrow."

"They moved it ahead."

Ellen catches a breath, ready to ask why, when Jana thunders up with the cart.

"My goodness," Ellen says, dropping her suitcase on it. "All that space for this one little bag."

Gravely, Jana considers the bag, then looks around at other passengers with their piled-up carts.

"How come you only have one, Gramma?"

"Well, it's easier that way," Ellen tells her. "Besides, it holds everything I really need. And if I need something else, I can get it here. I'll bet there are stores in Winnipeg, aren't there?"

Jana giggles.

"Tell you what. If I need anything, maybe you can come with me and help me find it?"

Jana glances at her father before answering.

"Sure. I help Mom lots when she goes shopping."

Stan smiles.

"Actually, she's a pretty good little shopper."

Stan swings Jana onto his shoulders and threads his way to the exit. There's no congestion at the parking lot and in minutes they're pulling away from the airport.

Stan flicks a glance ate Ellen. "Good flight?"

Ellen nods, then pauses. "I was just thinking how different this airport is. It was a zoo leaving home. It's all torn up for a new runway or something and parking is a nightmare."

He laughs. "Well, that's one of the nice things about living here. We're big enough to be a city but not big enough to have all the hassles you do out on the coast."

Stan clears his throat. "I thought I'd take you home and give you a chance to get settled while I slip out and see Joanne." His eyes slide sideways to meet hers.

Ellen understands what he's saying. "Sure. That's fine by me. Maybe I can even get dinner started."

Jana sings into the conversation.

"I know what's for dinner," she says. "Mommy's got a surprise for you."

Ellen starts to laugh. Kids and secrets. They can't wait to tell them.

"Then you better hush," she says, "Or it won't be a surprise anymore."

Jana starts to talk about something else. Ellen wishes for some way to talk to Stan, but there isn't one. Not with Jana sitting there. She listens patiently, enjoying the nearness of Jana and her bubbly radiance.

When they reach the house, Stan swings her bag out of the trunk, carries it to the porch, and opens the front door. Then he turns to Jana.

"Honey, I'm going back to the hospital to see how Lissy's doing. I'll tell Mommy that Grandma got here okay."

"Can I come too?" she asks.

"No, not this time. I thought you could look after Grandma till I get back."

Jana nods. "Okay."

Stan gives her a quick hug, then puts his hand on Ellen's shoulder.

"Thanks. Thanks for coming."

She's embarrassed. She hates it when people thank her unnecessarily.

"Off you go," she tells him. "Jana and I will be just fine. Maybe Joanne could phone me when she knows how things are going."

Ellen is mixed up in time and has to adjust her watch by two hours. It's mid-afternoon already and she hasn't had lunch yet.

"Are you hungry?" she asks Jana.

"We had lunch before we came to get you," she replies. "Daddy took me to Tim Hortons."

"Was it good?"

Jana thinks for a minute. "It was okay, but it wasn't as good as Mummy's."

Ellen gives her a hug.

If only all of life could be that simple.

— 8 —

JANA PRATTLES ON, JUMBLING comments and questions together in a way that usually delights Ellen, but today her words won't come into focus. Ellen's thoughts are with Lissy. She listens for the phone, making a hasty bargain with God, or the Earth Mother, or whoever is listening. If Joanne calls with good news — if the tumour is encapsulated — she'll give up her trip to California and do volunteer work at the Children's Hospital for a year. Two years. For the rest of her life, if that will make a difference. If the tumour is clean, the surgery will be quick and Joanne will call soon. "Please," she asks. "Let the call be soon."

Her neck tightens. A cold shiver ripples down her spine, roiling her stomach in a wave of nausea. Soon could be bad news too. The surgeons might discover it was so widespread they could do nothing. Soon could mean complications. But wait, there has to be a biopsy, doesn't there? Ellen is sure they do that while the patient is still on the operating table. The patient. She can't equate Lissy to "the patient," but she's pretty sure about the biopsy. That takes a little longer. Ellen draws upon scenarios based on nothing but wishes. She wants to receive a joyous phone call from Joanne. She wants to hear the tumour was not malignant, completely contained, and removed quickly and easily. She wants to know Lissy will be home soon, to be her own sweet self again. She wants the light to come back into her life.

Vaguely, she's aware that Jana's chatter has stopped and the little girl is gazing fixedly at her.

"Isn't that right, Gramma?" she asks, her face screwed up with concern.

Ellen drags her mind back into focus.

"I'm sorry, honey. Grandma's a little bit tired. I guess I wasn't listening very well. What did you say?"

Jana has trouble with the word *asked* and says it the way Shakespearean characters do, in two syllables — ask-ed. "I ask-ed you about Lissy," she says.

"What about Lissy, honey?"

"I said she was getting all better and then I ask-ed you wasn't that right and you didn't say anything."

The wide, innocent eyes look into Ellen's soul. She makes herself smile before she speaks.

"Of course she's going to get better," she says. "Then she can come home and tell us all about it."

Jana wrinkles her face in thought.

"But some people don't get better, do they? My other Gramma didn't get better. She went to the hospital and the doctor was going to fix her, but he couldn't. Daddy said it was 'cause she was old and tired, but Lissy isn't old and tired, is she?"

Ellen pulls her close and rocks her, stroking the wisps of kitten-soft hair, whispering kisses against her head.

"No, baby. Lissy isn't old and tired. She's going to be okay."

She clings to Jana for a long minute, then Jana's chubby hand pats her shoulder. The mantel clock chimes its melodious reminder that the afternoon is flitting away, breaking the moment like a pin puncturing a soap bubble.

"My goodness! It's five o'clock already! Let's look around the kitchen and see what we can make for dinner."

Jana pulls away. "I know! I know! Mummy already made it."

She continues to talk as she drags Ellen into the kitchen.

"Look," she crows, pulling open the fridge door. "There it is."

And there it is. Joanne's casserole stands ready to pop into the oven. A salad sparkles, colourful and crisp beneath its tightly-stretched Saran-wrap cover. A package of brown-and-serve buns sits nearby, ready to complete the meal. Trust Joanne. Always thinking ahead. Always trying to be ready for anything. Just this once, Ellen thinks, just this once she should have simply walked away and left it for someone else to do.

"I'm going to help you, Gramma," Jana announces. "I help Mummy lots. I put the knifes and forks on the table. I put the butter on, too."

"That's great," Ellen says. She squints at the post-it note on the casserole, and pops it into the microwave, listening to the musical beeps as she punches in the required setting. As it fills the room with its familiar hum, Ellen picks up the buns, peering at the label. She's never used them and debates whether they have to be baked in the stove oven or if they can go in the little toaster oven. She opts for the smaller oven, pops the buns in and turns it on.

"I don't think that's right, Gramma," Jana says, her small voice filled with concern. "Mummy always puts the oven on first so it gets hot."

"Hmmmh," Ellen replies, un-crumpling the wrapper and reading it more carefully. "Looks like Mummy was right. Let's just leave the oven on low so they can defrost and warm up. That way they'll taste almost as good as homemade."

"Now, Miss Jana," she says, while Jana giggles, "you can get busy with the silverware and I'll put the dishes on the table. How many plates will we need?"

"For just you and me or for Mummy and Daddy too?" she asks.

"For just you and me, I guess," Ellen replies.

Jana grimaces, wrinkling her lip in distaste.

"Gramma, that's too easy. I can count way morether than that."

Ellen's heart warms. That was a word Jana's mother used when she was little. If far and farther went together, so did more and morether.

"Okay, then. How many for you and me and Mummy and Daddy?"

The little girl beams.

"Four!" she announces, holding up four chubby fingers to make sure Ellen recognizes that she has the correct number.

"Good for you! Maybe we should set the table for four so it'll be all ready when Mummy and Daddy come home. But I don't think they'd want us to wait for them, do you?"

Jana agrees, and they busy themselves with the minutia of the meal. Ellen pops the buns into the now-warm oven, while Jana explains which of the salad dressings are Mummy's favourites and which are Daddy's favourites. She, herself, doesn't like any of them.

"So what do you put on your salad?" Ellen asks.

"This," Jana declares, reaching into the cupboard and plucking a jar from the shelf.

"Peanut butter?"

Gravely she nods her head. "It's really good."

"Jana, I think you're teasing me. We don't put peanut butter on salads."

"I do," she says. "Mummy said I could."

Ellen looks doubtfully at the jar of peanut butter.

"Jana, peanut butter doesn't pour. It just sits in globs. How do you put it on your salad?"

As she tries to imagine what Joanne might do to peanut butter to convert it to a salad dressing, Jana suddenly whirls and runs toward the front hall.

"Mummy's home!"

Somehow, she's heard the small sounds the car makes when it turns into the driveway. Seconds later the door opens. Stan and Joanne enter. Joanne drops to her knees, folding Jana to her, clutching her closely and rocking her gently.

Stan looks at Ellen, his hand on Joanne's shoulder, his eyes blank and dead. He shakes his head silently and looks toward the floor, fighting to keep himself under control.

The hug continues until Jana squirms away.

"Where's Lissy, Mummy? Is she all better yet?"

Joanne reaches out to hold Jana's hands before she speaks. "No, baby. Lissy isn't all better. Lissy is very sick and the doctor needs to keep her in the hospital for a while longer."

For once, Jana doesn't respond with her eternal "Why?" but accepts her mother's statement at face value.

"Me'n Gramma made dinner for you," she announces proudly. "I showed her where everything was and I helped her and everything."

Suddenly Stan's head snaps up. "What's that?"

Smoke!

Ellen and Joanne shout at the same moment. In the seconds it takes Joanne to rise to her feet, Ellen turns and dashes into the kitchen, where a plume of smoke streams from the toaster oven. There's a flurry of activity as she pulls the buns from the oven, Stan opens the back door and Joanne turns on the stove hood's venting fan.

"Darn it, I thought I could just brown those in the toaster oven instead of heating up the whole stove."

"It's okay, Mom," Joanne says. "I've got more buns in the freezer. It'll just take a couple of minutes."

"Here, honey. Give me your coat," Stan says to Joanne. "I'll hang it up for you."

While Jana is distracted, Ellen turns to Joanne and silently mouths Lissy's name. Joanne shakes her head. They'll talk later.

Jana chatters merrily through the meal, but neither Stan, Joanne, nor Ellen manage to eat much.

"Can I have a special ice cream?" Jana asks as dinner draws to a close.

Stan nods. "I'll get it for you." As he digs into the freezer compartment at the top of the fridge, he explains: "There's a little store in the shopping centre that makes specialty cones. They have a rocket cone and a couple of others, but Jana's favourite is the clown."

He brings out a small extravaganza of ice cream with a two-scoop body, licorice whip arms, piped ice-cream legs, and a sample-sized cone upside down on the top scoop, for a hat. The eyes are brown mini M&Ms, bright yellow M&Ms decorate the hat and others serve as buttons on the clown's suit.

Joanne takes it from him and gently removes the clear plastic covering.

"Did you want one, too?" he asks Ellen, reaching back into the freezer.

Ellen shakes her head. "I think I'll pass for now. I can probably put on pounds just looking at that."

We're at it again, she thinks. *Every time something goes wrong, we pretend nothing has happened.* As far back as she can remember, that's been the pattern. Who cares about ice cream clowns right now? She wants to know about Lissy. They've told her nothing, but she can read their body language. Something is terribly wrong.

Her mind continues to windmill. Jana's only a little girl, but she deserves the truth too. How long do they think they can make believe everything is okay? It's the same destructive pattern she and Al followed — never facing reality. For a moment she's tempted to break the bubble and ask a direct question, a question Stan and Joanne will have to answer. But she doesn't.

Later, after Jana has gone to bed, Ellen finally learns the truth.

"Lissy's got a neuroblastoma," Joanne says. "They couldn't get it all."

"What's a neuroblastoma?"

Stan gently takes over. "It's one of those malignancies that affect the sympathetic nervous system. If they'd caught it earlier, they might have had a chance. But it's too widespread now to do anything."

Joanne's head snaps up. "She still has a chance, Stan."

He reaches out and puts his hand on her shoulder.

Ellen is bewildered.

"How did it get so widespread? Has she been sick? I don't understand how it got this far without anyone noticing something was wrong."

Stan draws a deep breath before he answers.

"That's what makes the damned things so insidious. It's a silent tumour. It doesn't cause any symptoms. Youngsters don't complain, either verbally, or by being cranky, or any of the things kids usually do when something's wrong. There just aren't any symptoms.

"Joanne's the one who found it. She noticed that Lissy was developing a bit of a tummy. That happens with kids." He pauses. "Well, you know. You've had a family. Anyway, kids grow in spurts — they stretch out and get long and lanky, then they fill out before they shoot up again. Lissy stretched out and we thought she was just filling out. It was such a gradual thing. When Joanne got her some new clothes, she noticed they were tight around the tummy. The next time we got something for her, we realized she wasn't filling out all over, like she usually does. She was just getting a solid little paunch. Her arms and legs were normal, but she had this little pot on her.

"When Joanne felt her tummy, it was firm, like she'd been doing body building or something. That's when we began to wonder. It didn't take the doctor long to figure out what was happening."

Joanne takes up the thread.

"He found an abdominal mass and told us they'd have to do a surgical exploration. There were several other things it could have been, but the fact that there were no symptoms was the worst symptom of all."

There is a long pause before she continues.

"These things aren't always abdominal, but they're most common around the adrenal gland, near the kidney. That's where hers is. They thought it might have been a Wilm's tumour at first, but it wasn't. If it was encapsulated — nice and neatly contained — there was a good chance it could be removed and everything would be okay. But it wasn't. It was spread out and messy and invaded everything."

She stops.

Ellen can't believe what she's hearing. The two of them are so calm — as through they're giving a weather report.

"Isn't there anything they can do? What about chemotherapy? Or radiation?"

"That's what we have to decide," Stan says. "The chances are pretty much non-existent at this point, so we have to decide whether we want to put her through that with the odds so overwhelming that it won't do any good, and will just destroy whatever time she has left."

He looks directly at Ellen.

"Chemo and radiation aren't easy procedures. People have unreal notions about them. They're damned hard on you. They make you sicker than you've ever been in your life. And I'm not sure I want to put her through that. I could see it if there was any hope, but why torment her when it won't do any good?"

"You don't know that," Joanne snaps. "It's the only chance she's got. If we don't try it, she's going to die for sure."

He turns to face her.

"Joanne, we both love her. And we have since the day she was born. But this isn't about who loves her the most or about giving up. It's about Lissy and what's best for her. You heard the doctor. He said they could try radiation and chemo, but he wouldn't recommend it. We talked to other parents who've gone through the process. It was a pretty horrendous experience. And I remember a couple of them saying they wished they'd just let their child go in peace, rather than put them through so much torment."

Joanne's eyes are fixed on him. Her face has turned to stone. He steps closer and gently pulls her toward him. She shudders, pushing him away.

"You say you love her. Then help me fight for her. Yes, it's going to be hard. I know that. But she's young. She's got resilience. She can bounce back. We've both seen that. And doctors can be wrong."

She takes a deep breath, trying to stop the sobs that creep around the edges of her voice. "Stan, we've got to give her whatever chance there is."

Silence hangs like a curtain between them. Abruptly, Stan turns to Ellen.

"What do you think, Mom?"

She's taken aback and gropes for words. "I ... I don't know what to say, Stan. I understand what you're saying — radiation and chemo can be terrible. But I see Joanne's point too. If it's Lissy's only hope, is it fair to withhold, even if it might not do any good?"

"That's my point," he replies. "It isn't even a faint hope. The doctor as good as told us that. So why torture her when it won't do any good? What's the point of that? Let's make it decent for her and make her last days comfortable."

"You don't know that. You don't know it won't do any good. And that's not what the doctor said. He said he couldn't guarantee results. That doesn't mean there won't be any. You're a quitter, Stan. Well, I won't let us quit on Lissy. I'm going to make sure she has those treatments if it's the last thing I do!"

They stand immobile, fighting cocks waiting for the split second to fly in and plant their spurs in each other.

Ellen takes one of their hands in each of her own.

"Please, Joanne, Stan. Don't freeze each other out right now. I can't help you because I don't know enough about it. In any case, this is your decision. But listen to each other. This isn't about who wins an argument. It's about what's best for Lissy. Let's think of her."

Joanne speaks first. "Believe me, Mother, it's Lissy I'm thinking about."

Stan takes a deep breath. "She's my daughter, too," he says, his voice oddly gentle.

Ellen looks from one to the other. "Is there anything I can say?"

Joanne shakes her head, but it's Stan who speaks.

"I don't think there's anything anyone can say at this point."

The sudden peal of the telephone interrupts the moment. Stan and Joanne look at each other. The phone rings again and still they stand, frozen in a nightmare tableau.

"Isn't anyone going to answer that?" Ellen asks, as it rings for a third and fourth time.

Slowly, Stan turns on his heel and picks up the phone. The conversation is over in moments.

Numbly, he puts the receiver down and turns to Joanne.

"She's gone," he whispers. "Lissy's gone."

Ellen doesn't want to be there at that moment. She doesn't want to see the raw agony that erupts. But most of all she doesn't want to see the anger that boils up in Joanne and spills over both of them.

"She didn't have to die," Joanne says. "They could have helped her but you wouldn't let them."

Stan's arms reach out. "Joanne," he begins.

"No. Don't touch me. Just leave me alone."

She whirls and runs from the room. Stan's arms hang awkwardly in mid-air, twin branches deformed by wind and torn by storms. His eyes close as his arms slowly drop, brought down by a weight he cannot bear.

※

The next morning Stan and Joanne leave for the hospital. There are things to attend to that Ellen can't even imagine. They throw themselves into planning Lissy's funeral, insisting it isn't going to be a funeral but a celebration of her life. Lissy will be cremated. There won't be a church service, but a memorial for her friends and family. What they want, Stan says, is to recreate the sense of Lissy's life. He sits through hours of home-videos, looking for clips of the smiling, pretty little girl as she grows from a baby to a toddler, to a proud kindergarten graduate, and then sets out on her first day of "real" school.

The journey isn't very long.

Jana is confused.

"Isn't Lissy ever coming back, Gramma?"

"No, honey. Lissy isn't. But she'll always be in our hearts."

Jana shakes her head. "No. I want her in my house." Tears brim in her eyes. "Didn't she like living here?"

"Oh, baby," Ellen cries, sweeping her into an embrace. "Of course she liked living here."

"Then why did she go away? Was she mad at me?"

Inside, Ellen seethes. Damn Joanne and Stan anyway. They're being so level-headed, so calm, cool, and collected. They're so reasonable in their responses that Jana doesn't realize what has actually happened. Ellen knows pre-schoolers don't have a real grasp on the concept of death, but they're making it sound as though Lissy has just gone away, as someone might leave a friend's house and go play somewhere else. Jana is translating that as leaving, as one might after a quarrel, or the way Lissy sometimes stamped into her room and shut the door when she didn't want Jana to play with her toys.

"No, honey, she wasn't mad at you. She loved you. You were her sister, her only sister. You were really, really special to her."

"Then why won't she come back?"

There is no answer.

— 9 —

AL'S ARRIVAL SURPRISES ELLEN, although she realizes it shouldn't. He's still Lissy's grandfather. No, he *was* Lissy's grandfather. Lissy is gone. Her mind shies from the thought, a skittish colt spooked by a shadow. She can't yet accept the unchangeable fact.

Al is alone, and she's thankful for that. They're oddly formal in their greetings, more like casual acquaintances that haven't seen each other for a while than people who shared the greater part of their lives with each other and co-parented four children.

"How are you?" he asks.

"Fine, thanks. And you?"

He shakes his head. "I'm getting old, Ellie. Just plain getting old. I'm not ready for this. I don't know how to handle it."

Impulsively, she grabs his hand. "Me neither."

He squeezes back, then loosens his grip. Ellen goes back into neutral when, unexpectedly, his arm slides around her waist, drawing her into a hug. Their bodies still fit together. They fit too well. She relaxes against him for a minute before drawing back.

"Hey, we're not doing that any more. Remember? Besides, what would your girlfriend say?"

He makes an Al face — a funny thing he does with his mouth. Half goes up and half goes down while his eyebrows do a little dance of their own.

"She's history, Ellie."

It's her turn to be surprised.

"I'm sorry," she tells him. And to her astonishment, she really means it.

He reaches his arm out again, but she slides away, leaving only her hand. He holds it for a minute before turning it over and stroking the back of it, as one would stroke a kitten. His touch is a soft cincture: a single strand of spider web, drifting on warm summer air. But, she remembers, a strand of spider web is stronger than a strand of steel. She stands, tense and wary, a small animal venturing too close to a trap. She forces herself to relax. There is no trap. She's no longer bound to him, no longer at his beck. She is no longer part of "Al'n'Ellen."

He closes both hands over hers, an envelope that holds her motionless as he peers at her with warm eyes. Ellen stifles the urge to laugh. He reminds her of a big puppy dog.

"She wasn't you, Babe."

They stand for another moment while she searches for a way to defuse the situation, but he makes the move first. He drops her hand, half turns away, and brushes his hair back as though he's just come through a wind tunnel.

"Ellie, what's happening with Joanne and Stan? They're hurting mega, but I can't figure out what's gone wrong. When they need each other most they act like they're on separate planets. It breaks me up to see them like this."

"I know. She blames him for not letting them try radiation and chemo. It wouldn't have made any difference; Lissy was gone before they ever had the chance to try it, but Joanne can't accept that.

"He's upset because ..." her voice catches. It takes a minute to get herself under control. "Al, I don't know why they're like they are. I know they had an argument about the chemo just before Lissy died, but I think that was just pouring gas on a fire that was already smouldering. There's more going on than we know about. Neither one is asking for our help, and it's hard to know what to do without intruding. I don't know what to say to either of them."

Her throat tightens. She tries to continue talking, but the words are forced. It physically hurts to speak. Al leans closer to hear. "We don't know the whole story, and my guess is, we never will."

He nods, slowly, reluctantly. His hands make futile gestures.

"I don't know how to help them either."

At that moment, Jana bounds into the room, shattering the brittle space between them. She rushes forward to claim her grandfather, grabbing his hand, tugging him away.

"Whoa there, chickadee. Where are we going in such a hurry?"

"Come see, Grampa," Jana pleads. "It's reeal special."

"Reeal, reeal special?" Al echoes.

"It really, really is," she promises, her wide eyes a mirror of his own. "You can come too, Gramma."

Al grins. "Come on, Babe. Looks like a command performance."

They follow Jana, expecting to go into one of the other rooms, but she leads them outside, onto the back deck. As they reach the door she turns and puts a chubby finger to her lips.

"You have to be real quiet or he'll go away."

They step carefully through the door, closing the screen gently behind them so as not to frighten the elusive whatever-it-is.

Jana stops, triumphantly, lowers her voice to a whisper, and points.

"See. It's a kingbird!"

It's a bird, but Ellen has never heard it called a kingbird. Al's eyes catch hers and points of laughter dance between them.

"That's a blue jay, Jana," Al whispers.

The tousled head shakes vigorously.

"No, it isn't," she insists. "Look. He's got a crown on top of his head. He's special."

"Maybe he's king of the blue jays," Al suggests.

Ellen's eyes roll upward. Is this pandering or what? A Stellar jay is, after all, just a talkative bird with some blue feathers. But Al is happy to go along with Jana's decision that this bird is somehow special. Still, king of the blue jays?

Jana considers the idea.

"Maybe. He's lots special. He eats peanuts, too."

Al looks at Ellen with a wicked smile. "That's pretty special, all right."

They both know jays will eat anything that isn't nailed down and they're sharing a memory of a time when the kids were young and their holidays were spent camping — tents, smoky fires, the works. A flock of jays raided their camp and almost cleaned them out. Swooping over the table, they inhaled a bowl of popcorn, another of potato chips, then moved on to gobble up hot dogs, the buns the hot dogs were going into. They cleaned up a plate of Ritz crackers for good measure. As an encore they made off with a pot scrubber, one of a pair of dice Al was using in a Parcheesi game, and a chunk of incense-like mosquito coil set on the table but not yet lighted. From the way the jays scooped things up, it might not have mattered it if had been burning. Fastidious they were not. Ellen grins back at Al, acknowledging the memory. She's about to make a comment, but Al reads her mind and shakes his head.

He's right. If Jana wants to think jays are special, so be it. And if she needs to believe that this particular jay is especially talented because he eats peanuts, there's no harm in that. Al believes kids should have fantasies. Ellen used to think it was kinder to demolish them, teach them about the real world, as her parents did, making sure she and her brother never entertained illusions about wee folk, ghosts, spooks, and goblins, never believed in Halloween, the Tooth Fairy, or Santa Claus. Now she's not so sure. Maybe kids need fantasies. Grownups, too. She's tired of living in a world where everything has to be verified for content and political correctness.

＊

Dinner is a painful affair. Joanne and Stan are excruciatingly polite with one another. It's difficult to carry on a conversation when you can talk to one or the other, but not with both. Ellen soon tires of the three-legged round robin.

After dinner a man from the funeral home arrives to discuss the service for Lissy. Al and Ellen are shunted into the background as he talks with Stan and Joanne. He begins by asking for their suggestions for the service. Stan corrects him immediately.

"We don't want a funeral service. We want … a celebration of her life."

Ellen bites her lips fiercely, trying to hold back tears. How can you celebrate Lissy's all-too-short life? What is there in death that calls for celebration?

The man is unconcerned. He bows his head momentarily, as though deep in thought, or perhaps deep in prayer. It's hard to tell. Ellen is sure he's heard it all before and is simply letting Stan have his say. After a moment, he looks up and nods, obsequiously, condescendingly, silently telling them that he knows best. Then he begins promoting his product. What kind of coffin do they want? Live music or taped? Who will give the eulogy? Which members of the family will speak? If they don't have a family minister, he has a list of people who can perform non-denominational services. There is an adjoining room that can be rented for a reception after the service, and caterers who can look after the reception. He has lists upon lists upon lists. He's done this a hundred times. Ellen hates him. How can anyone be so inured to death? Especially the death of a child?

Ellen wants to scream, tell him to get out and leave them alone. This isn't the time for the Resurrection and the Life. It's time for a picnic on a hilltop to remember a sweet little girl who shouldn't have left them so soon.

Stan is no help. It's obvious he's trying to patch up the quarrel with Joanne by deferring to her every decision. She chooses not to understand what he's doing — or at least that's how it seems. Ellen knows her daughter. Despite her grief, Joanne knows exactly what's going on and she's playing volleyball with a barbed wire net.

Eventually, the interview ends. The man leaves. Jana is tucked away in bed. Stan and Joanne head for their bedroom, leaving Al and Ellen alone in the front room. They arrange themselves on the chesterfield, facing the television.

"Anything special you want to watch?" he asks.

She shakes her head.

He clicks on something and turns the volume down. It's audio wallpaper, covering up the silence in the room.

Once again he reaches for her hand. She lets him take it.

"How's it been for you, Babe?" he asks, watching her closely.

"Okay, I guess. I'm getting along."

"I'm glad," he says. "I still worry about you."

"Isn't it lucky you don't have to anymore," she retorts, pulling her hand away.

His hand remains outstretched.

"That's okay, Babe. I understand. I treated you pretty badly and you're entitled to a few barbs."

This is definitely not the Al she used to know. The silence is thinned by the low murmur of sound from the television.

"How about you? How are you getting along?"

He takes a minute to respond.

"Okay, I guess. It's funny, but things are better since Verna left."

Verna? Ellen's so used to thinking of her as "Al's Bimbo" or the "Vestal Virgin" that she forgets for a minute who Verna is.

"What happened?"

He shrugs his shoulders in a gesture of renunciation.

"Nothing really happened, I guess."

Another pause.

"Well, that's not quite true. What happened is I suddenly realized she wasn't you. She never would be. She never gave me any space. I guess I liked your style better, Ellie."

He recaptures her hand.

"Al, don't you think it's a little late for all this? I mean, it's over. We're history."

She's uncomfortable with the direction this conversation is taking.

"I'm serious, Al," she repeats, with as much force as she can muster without being rude. "We're history. Period. End of an era. That's it. There ain't no more."

He ignores her.

"Babe, this isn't the time or the place. There's too much going on right now. But later, once this is over, can we get together to talk? Just talk. That's all."

She agrees this is neither the time nor the place. She's not sure she agrees they have anything to talk about, but there's no harm in talking. At least, she hopes there isn't.

"Okay. That can happen. After this is over — when we're both back home again."

It's an exit line if she ever heard one. She seizes it and rises to her feet.

"Good night, Al. See you in the morning."

❋

The week is one Ellen wishes she could forget. It ends with Lissy's service. The small chapel, crowded with friends and family, is filled with the cloying scent of funeral flowers. Ellen finds it hard to breathe. Jennifer sits beside her sister, along with Geoff and Robby. Stan's dad, his sisters and their families cluster together. There are friends from the neighbourhood, Lissy's godparents, and people Ellen doesn't recognize, but it doesn't matter. The service is a tear-jerker. Surely asking them to sing Sunday school hymns is going too far. There should be an edict prohibiting singing *Jesus Loves Me* at a child's funeral. And another to prohibit the reading of Ecclesiastics: *There is a time to live and a time to die.* It sounds strange without the thump of a guitar in the background and a chorus singing, "Turn, turn, turn." What she really wants is to prohibit funerals like this, or rather the need for funerals like this. Kids shouldn't die.

After, people gather in the reception room over cookies and coffee and tell each other what a beautiful service it was, and how meaningful it was. Even as her face freezes in the rictus that masquerades as a smile, she finds herself asking questions: Was it meaningful, and if so, to whom? If the point was to comfort those who Lissy left behind, it wasn't.

If it was to score points for the funeral director, it probably was. There was the mandatory picture of Lissy at the front of the chapel, a painful reminder that they'd never see that bright and bubbly little person again. She'd never bring sunlight and dewdrops and butterflies into their day with her smile. Her skipping rope, arranged casually on the table beside the picture, was a reminder that never again would Lissy come tripping down the stairs, bounce through hopscotch squares, or splash through puddles.

Everything, every word, every song, every object, is loaded with sentimentality and symbolism. And none of it represents Lissy. Not in Ellen's mind.

Ellen promises that she'll make her own farewell to Lissy at some other time, in some other place. Meanwhile, Lissy is still very much alive in her heart.

Al and the other kids stay until the weekend. Then they have to get back to work. A friend of the family shuttles Jennifer, Robby, and Geoff to the airport at various times for their various flights. Joanne makes her goodbyes at home. Each departure takes something from her, chipping away at the façade she's presented during the week. Finally, it's time for Al to go. Joanne surprises them by suggesting they all go together to see him off. They gather awkwardly around the van as Stan unlocks it and Al opens the middle door, then freeze when it reveals two boosters seats. No one says anything. No one moves, until Stan breaks the tableau, stepping forward to unlatch one from its secure position and stow it in a far corner of the garage.

Jana breaks the silence.

"Come on, Grampa," she says, tugging his hand. "You sit by the window and I'll sit in the middle by side of you and Gramma." She beams at them. She has a grin that's hard to resist and Ellen doesn't try.

Al quirks his eyebrows and she nods in reply. He gives her hand a squeeze before turning back to Jana.

"Okay, bright eyes," he says. "Let's get in."

They arrange themselves across the seat as Joanne and Stan slip quietly into their seats and buckle themselves in.

Jana chirps and chatters all the way to the airport, burbling merrily to everyone. When they reach the airport, Al calls out to Stan: "Don't bother parking. Just drop me off at the front. There's no sense coming in with me, because I'm just going to check my bag through and go straight to the departure lounge."

Joanne starts to object, but Al overrules her.

"No. I hate standing around saying goodbye."

As they pile out of the van, Al retrieves his bag and it's time for hugs all around. Ellen's comes last.

"I meant what I said, Babe," he tells her, his voice soft in her ear so no one else can hear. "I'll call you in a couple of days."

Ellen nods. She's not sure she should encourage him. It's over with them. Finished. Dead and gone. Bad choice of words. Over and done with. That's better. But while the inside of her head is holding back, the outside is nodding up and down like the puppet she's been all her life. Sure, dear. Yes, dear. Of course, dear. Whatever you say, dear.

Ah, well. Time to deal with that problem when she gets back. Right now it's more important to bring this scene to an end, to get Al off on his plane. And tomorrow, to catch her plane. Maybe then Stan and Joanne can find a time and a place to sit down and talk about whatever is tearing them apart. It becomes more painfully clear with each moment that the barrier between them, which neither has yet acknowledged, is growing higher, wider, and deeper.

Stan spends the remainder of the day shuttling between his den and the basement. Joanne moves between the kitchen and Lissy's room. They take unusual care not to be in the same place at the same time.

Jana stays glued to Ellen's side. They dress and undress her dolls. Ellen makes little folded paper hats for Jana, for the dolls, and for herself. She suggests making some new clothing for the dolls. Jana is enchanted. As far as she knows, dolls and their clothing come from a store.

Ellen hunts in Joanne's rag bag and finds a few scraps of printed material that she converts into elastic-waist dirndl skirts for the doll family.

"Gramma, can we make some for Lissy's dolls, too?" Jana asks.

She holds her breath for a minute before she can answer.

"Maybe later, sweetheart," she says. Jana knows Lissy is gone, but doesn't yet understand exactly what that means. Ellen isn't in a space dispassionate enough to explain it any further. It will have to be acquired knowledge that will gradually bring her to the truth. Ellen might have done something different if Stan or

Joanne had been in a more normal space, but they aren't, so she doesn't. The coward's way out. Do nothing and things might get better.

Dinner that night is another painfully polite meal. Words fly around the table: flights of little dickey birds, never really coming to rest anywhere, just batting endlessly around and around. They cover the silence but don't count as conversation.

The next day it's Ellen's turn to be driven to the airport. Stan has gone back to work.

"I wish you could stay longer, Mom," Joanne says.

"I wish I could, too, but you have things to do that I'm no part of. And Jana's going to need some special attention for a while. One of these days she's going to realize her sister isn't coming back. Ever."

"I know. It's just that … I'm so confused right now, Mom. I don't know what to think or what to do."

Ellen reaches toward her. Maybe this is the moment she's been waiting for, the moment when Joanne lowers her guard and will talk about what's gone wrong. Magically, Ellen will offer the suggestion Joanne's been waiting for. Things will be set right again, go back to where they used to be. Ellen's arm stretches out to Joanne, but instead of letting her mother enfold her, instead of moving into the protective circle of that arm, Joanne takes her mother's hand and holds it firmly. It's a defensive gesture — soft, gentle, but still keeping her at bay.

She takes a deep breath. "I guess I'll just have to figure it out for myself."

"Joanne …" Ellen stops. She doesn't know how to say what she wants to tell her. "Joanne, give yourself some room. You and Stan both need a little time. You're both upset right now. Don't do anything you're going to regret."

Joanne looks at her mother for a long moment.

"It's okay. I'm not making a sudden decision."

Ellen thinks she is taking her advice and feels relieved. She'll discover later that Joanne was simply telling her, in that oblique way she sometimes uses, that she's already made up her mind.

There's a last hug with Jana and it's time to go.

"Mom, you really should get an answering machine," Joanne calls as Ellen walks down the corridor to the departure lounge.

Ellen turns.

"That's one of the advantages of getting old. You don't have to do what other people think you should any more. I've decided to be eccentric. A Luddite. And don't go sending me one for Christmas. I won't use it."

For just a moment, Ellen can see the child in Joanne as she laughs at her mom. She steps through the gates, leaving Joanne and Jana behind.

The flight home is uneventful. She's thankful the seat beside her remains empty. She flips through the pages of a magazine to give her hands something to do. What she really wants to do is think, to find a solution. Stan and Joanne are in trouble. That much is evident. Joanne didn't want to talk about it, but from what she didn't say, it was easy to guess they'd been having problems for some time. Lissy's death was a catalyst, but not the cause of what was happening. Has Stan been seeing someone else? It didn't seem likely. He isn't really the type. Has Joanne met someone else? Again, it didn't seem likely, but perhaps she has her maternal blinkers on.

Ellen doesn't think they're having money problems. Stan earns a good income. Still, things aren't always what they seem. Neither said anything that offered an insight. Briefly, she wonders if history is repeating itself; if they don't communicate any better with each other than she and Al did — or, more accurately, didn't — there were serious problems ahead.

Jana is the one who generates the most concern. She's a sweet little girl who's at that wonderful age when questioning begins. There are lots of *whys* in her vocabulary as she sorts out her world, but not the important questions. Those will come later. What she needs right now is unconditional love from both her parents. Once the reality of Lissy's death hits home, she has to be reassured that she was in no way responsible. That she is still loved.

Ellen worries that given their present states of mind, neither Joanne nor Stan will even recognize Jana's concerns. Kids don't usually come out in the open and say what's bothering them. Sometimes they don't even know. You have to look behind their actions to figure out what's going on. And in the Glacier City that her daughter and son-in-law currently occupy, Ellen isn't the least bit sure that's going to happen.

Ellen hops a bus home, extricates the fistful of junk mail crammed into her mail box, and heads for her apartment.

Her bike is waiting. It draws her eyes, like a puppy dog that meets you at the door. She's sure it's asking to go out for a ride.

"It's a little too late right now," she murmurs. Then she stops. Why is it too late? She gained time on the flight home. It's just mid-afternoon. After the tensions of the past week, a ride would feel wonderful. It takes only moments to dig her biking clothes out of her dresser.

Fifteen minutes later, she's on the road. It feels good. She heads for a hill — suddenly she feels the need to sweat. Halfway up she realizes the ten days away have exacted a toll. It's a much harder ride than she remembers. It's time to honk, to stand up on the pedals and pump hard. Her feet bite into the bike pedals, pressing urgently against them as she levers herself into a standing position and powers her way up the hill. Her breath rasps and her lungs burn, but it helps ease the deeper pain. This hill has a designated bike lane, so she doesn't have to elbow for position with cars. There's enough latitude to spin the front wheel from one side to the other, reducing the grade from a straight climb to a diagonal slant. Still, it becomes harder and harder to maintain forward momentum. Her gluteus clenches with painful hardness as she strains against the pedals, willing them to turn, watching the slow passage of the tire treads crossing in front of the fender.

An hour later she's home again and headed for the shower. The blessed, soothing ease of hot water pours over her body, massaging the sore spots and unknotting tightened muscles.

There's still time to shop, restock her depleted fridge, and do all the other things that need doing. But she's glad she went for a ride first. Ellen pats the bike, as she might pat a faithful horse or a good dog. It's silly, but she doesn't care. Here, her actions don't have to be defended.

Half an hour later, as she towels her hair dry, the phone rings.

She half expects it to be Joanne, making sure she got home safely. Is this a turnaround for the nights Ellen used to wait for Joanne to arrive home from dates? But it isn't. The voice takes her by surprise.

"Hi, Babe. I hoped I could catch you. I phoned earlier, but you don't have an answering machine."

"Hi, Al." She's damned if she's going to defend her lack of an answering machine to him. Or even acknowledge it.

"Have a good flight?"

"Yes, thank you." What can you say about a plane flight? Nothing uneventful happened. The weather was calm. It was just a flight.

"What I'm calling for — I wondered if it would be okay if I came over for a while?"

If he came over for a while? Why on earth would he want to do that?

She doesn't want to wallow in Lissy's death with Al. That's something she'll work through in her own way, on her own terms, in her own time. There's nothing else left to talk about.

"Just for a little while," he says, as though he's read her mind.

Habit kicks in again. There's no reason for him not to come — other than her misgivings. Or that she doesn't want him to come. Or that she's never learned to say no to him.

"Uh … sure. That would be fine."

"Maybe I could pick up a pizza on the way over? Are you doing anything for dinner? We could go out somewhere if you'd rather."

"No. No. That's fine. I don't want to go out. Pizza will be great."

"Okay. I'll be there in about an hour."

Her eyes fly around the apartment. What needs to be done? Dusting? Vacuuming? What needs to be put away?

Forget it, she tells herself. *Whatever he wants, he isn't coming to inspect the place.* In truth, she's surprised he even knows where it is. His cheque goes directly into her bank account each month, not mailed to her home. Still, it wouldn't have been difficult for him to get her address from one of the kids.

She takes another look around the place. The suitcase is still sitting on a chair. Quickly, she moves to pick it up. Then she stops and sets it back down again.

"I can have a suitcase on the chair if I want to," she says, to no one in particular. "This is *my* home."

For good measure, she finishes rubbing her hair dry and drops the damp towel on top of the suitcase. Then she picks it up. There's no point in getting the suitcase wet just to annoy Al. She spreads it over the bathroom hamper and finds a dry towel to hang on the rack. It doesn't match, but she doesn't care.

By the time Al and his pizza arrive, she's feeling like a cat with its back arched and ready to spit. All it will take is one wrong word, but the word never comes. It turns out to be a pleasant evening. Whatever it was he wanted to talk about, he doesn't seem inclined to bring it up right now. They finish the pizza, she puts on a pot of coffee, and they ramble idly through an odd conversation.

He's doing well. He's thinking of renovating the house — expanding the half bath in the basement to a full bathroom. "It would be better for the kids if they come to visit," he says. "They could use the rec room like an apartment."

"Are they planning to visit?" she asks.

He shrugs. "Not that I know of, but better to get it done before they come."

"Don't you think they'd rather stay in their old rooms instead of moving down into the rec room?"

Again the shrug. "Well, that's okay if they're by themselves, I guess, but if they come with their families it isn't going to be too convenient."

She looks at him. "Al, Joanne is the only one who has a family. The others aren't even married yet. It's going to be a long, long time before you have to worry about accommodating a whole bunch of people."

He grins.

"Well, yeah. I guess you're right. I've just been thinking about it and I thought I should run it past you before I did anything."

She's not the least bit interested in what he does with the house, she realizes. He can bulldoze it down for all she cares.

But he isn't finished yet. "I mean, I know you've got a lot of emotional stock invested there, and I wouldn't want to hurt your feelings or anything like that, so I just thought I'd … um … kind of float the idea by you and see what you thought."

Emotional stock? In a hypothetical bathroom?

"That's very considerate, Al, but it really doesn't matter to me. If that's what you want to do, then go right ahead and do it."

He mulls that one over. "What I mean is, I guess I wondered if you might sort of look at the plans and help me figure out what I should put in there. You know, tiles and colours and that sort of thing."

Ellen looks at him.

"Al, there are only so many ways I can say this. I'm not living in that house. I'm not *going* to live in that house. It truly doesn't matter to me what you put in there. Just do whatever pleases you."

He gives her that look again, the one that says, *I hear the words you're saying but I'm having some difficulty with them because they aren't the words I expect you to say and, in my greater wisdom, I know you don't really mean them.*

"Honestly, Al," she adds, as if she hopes a little extra emphasis will get her point across.

"In fact," she continues, "I guess I'm surprised that you're even planning to stay there. I mean, it's an awfully big house for one person."

He nods agreement.

"Well, yeah, sometimes it is. But I'm used to it, you know how it is."

She shakes her head.

"No, I really don't. That size of a house takes a lot of looking after. And one person doesn't really need all that room. It was too big when just the two of us lived there. That was something I always hoped we'd do once the kids left — sell it and get a smaller place that would be easier to look after. But it never quite worked out."

"Jeez, Babe. I never knew you felt that way about it. I remember how sentimental my Mom was about her house. She never wanted to change anything.

"I guess what I remember best is that you could always depend on things to be the same. Like the Christmas tree — it was always in the same place. And the coffee table was always in front of the fireplace. And the big coat tree was always in the front hall, just beside the door. Remember that coat tree, Babe?"

Indeed she did. It was the ugliest coat tree she'd ever seen. The story was that Al's mother wanted a coat tree for the front hall and had in mind a shiny brass tree full of scrolls and curves and bright reflections. Al's father spotted this one at an auction one day and bought it for two dollars. It looked like it might have come from a schoolroom somewhere, possibly around the turn of the century — old enough to be ugly but not quite right for an antique. It was made of heavy dark wood with heavy metal hooks. No graceful scrolls, no gleaming brass. No sleekly designed hangers, just metal hooks in staggered rows to accommodate six coats, cloaks, hats, or whatever they were designed to hold in those long-ago days when the thing was new.

Al's mother hated it. From the minute she first laid eyes on it, she hated it. But Al's father had bought it and placed it in the front hall, so that was that. Even after his father died, the monstrosity stayed there. It stayed until she died, years later. When they moved, Al wanted to bring it to their new house, but Ellen refused. It was one of the few times she'd put her foot down and vetoed one of his suggestions. Her stand generated a three-day sulk, but she didn't care. Eventually, he got over it. Each time Ellen entered their front hall, she was happy not to see it there.

Looking back, there was a lesson to be learned. The world didn't end when she said no. It didn't even quiver. Her mind reverts to the present. The notion of Al spending weekends vacuuming, dusting, and doing housekeeping things doesn't reconcile itself with the man she lived with for all those years. But of course, she reminds herself, the Bimbo probably looked after all that while she was there.

She realizes he's still talking and tunes back in.

"Since Verna left, I have a cleaning service in every other week. Doesn't cost that much and it isn't like one person makes that much of a mess."

Ellen's hands busy themselves stacking things on the table.

"There's still a chunk of pizza left," she says. "Would you like to take it home with you? Maybe for lunch or something?"

"No, that's fine. You keep it."

"No, thank you. It's far too much for me. I don't usually eat pizza, and I don't think I can handle it two days in a row."

"Okay. If you're sure you don't want it."

Oh, please! She thinks. Let's not go through this gavotte over a chunk of leftover pizza.

She stands abruptly.

"I've got some aluminum foil. I'll wrap it up for you."

"Okay, thanks. Then I can just pop it in the microwave."

She laughs. "Al, you know darn well you can't just pop it in the microwave. You've nuked a hundred pieces of pizza and you've never used foil on any of them. Don't start getting helpless at this stage of your life."

He smiles.

"*Touché.* In that case, could you wrap it in Saran so I don't have to put it in something else first?"

"I can. I'll even put it on a paper plate first."

Despite the cheerfulness of their banter, she's cross with herself. She doesn't know why she's even bothering to do this. It makes more sense just to leave it in the box it came in. But, no, she's looking for an exit line and offering to wrap up the leftovers is a graceful one.

At last, Al picks up the clue, gathers his pizza, and leaves with a big smile and a friendly hug.

"It was good to see you again, Babe."

He glances around.

"Nice place you've got here. But then, you've always had good taste."

Ellen almost laughs out loud. If she had such good taste, how come she ended up married to him?

— 10 —

THE DAYS SLIDE BY. Ellen hears from Al at intervals. She rides, ignoring threatening skies and blustery winds, trying to make up for lost time. Her legs and lungs complain. Her seat breaks out in rebellious blisters. She should know better. She *does* know better.

"I know you can't make up for lost time," she mutters. "Once it's gone, it's gone forever, but why does it take so long to catch up?"

Her muscles aren't fooled. They grumble during the day, twitch and flex during the long, restless nights. But still she rides. Months pass. Holidays flit by, unnoticed and uncelebrated.

She phones Joanne as often as she dares, inventing such transparent reasons to call that Joanne finally breaks into laughter.

"Mom, I'm okay. You don't have to worry. I promise I'll call if I need you."

"Okay. Then I won't call again, unless …"

"Unless nothing," Joanne interrupts. "I know you love me, and I love you too. But you don't have to call twice a week."

Ellen has a love-hate relationship with her phone. At times she resents it heartily. It rings at the wrong times, and doesn't ring when she wants it to. She's fed up with endless busy signals. Call waiting is even worse. She hates thinking that someone is measuring the importance of her call by putting her on hold while they talk to someone else. She hates the music they play, and hates even more the inane announcements that interrupt the music.

She is driven to distraction by people seemingly talking to themselves in the stores, on the streets, at the bus stop, when they are really talking into cell phones.

"I'm not eavesdropping," she tells herself. "They talk so loud you can't help but hear. And most of it is so stupid."

She has no patience with aimless conversations. Joanne is like her in that way, but both Geoff and Robbie thrive on long, floating discussions. It doesn't seem to matter who they talk to, they go on for hours at a time. When they were still home, they were far worse than the girls about tying up the phone line. Ellen's friends laughed when she complained. In their homes, it was daughters, not sons, who monopolized the phone.

"I should be so lucky," they'd tell her, winking at each other.

When Robbie lived at home and Geoff moved away, they found solace in calling each other. Later, she'd ask what they talked about. Not directly, but casual comments, like: "So, what's new with Geoff?" There was never a definite answer. It seemed as though another level of communication was going on that had nothing to do with words. It should have been the twins who were that close, she thought.

Jennifer is somewhere in between. She starts well, then partway through a conversation Ellen can almost hear the gears changing and a display screen flashing the message "Enough!"

Joanne phones later in the week and puts Jana on the line. Jana loves to talk — about everything and everybody. All Ellen has to do is listen.

Then Joanne comes back on the line. "Mom, don't worry about me. We're working through this. I'll write you next week. Okay?"

"Okay," she agrees, then adds, "Does this mean I don't have to get an answering machine?"

Joanne laughs. Thank the gods for that little spark. Maybe things will work out after all.

"And spoil your birthday surprise?" she flips back. They hang up, a mutual smile singing over the wires. Joanne doesn't mention Stan. Ellen doesn't ask.

Ellen writes careful letters to Jennifer, Geoffrey, and Robby, asking them to be especially attentive to Joanne for the next little while.

"Even if you have nothing to say," she writes, "she needs to hear from you. No matter what you say on paper, your letter tells her you care and that she has her family behind her."

Ellen pictures the groans that will elicit. "There's Mom," Jennifer will quip. "Psych 101 and holding." The boys will complain she's watching too many daytime talk shows. They'll laugh at her insistence on writing letters instead of phoning. They might even phone Joanne and laugh about it with her. No matter. Whatever they do, the response will help Joanne.

Now it's time to get her own life back on track.

"There's no reason why I can't go ahead with my plans for California," she tells her image in the mirror as she brushes her teeth, gurgling around the froth of toothpaste in her mouth. It's still a goal. A dream. Her wish-upon-a-star. She's entitled. Cancelling the trip won't help Lissy. It won't make any difference to Jana. Unless something changes drastically, it won't make things either better or worse for Joanne.

She spits, then rinses her mouth.

"The only one it will affect is me."

Her mirrored image nods and she smiles as she pulls on her riding gear. She looks forward to riding. Her body needs it now. Her head needs it, too. She suspects she's become addicted, but she doesn't care. There's a wonderful freedom on the bike. Nothing matters but Ellen and the road: How to get around the next bend. Which gear to use for this little hill. Which gear for that larger hill. When to start pumping extra hard. When to ease off.

She's learned to stretch as she pedals, staving off the cramps and soreness that once plagued her. She's learned a lot and it's been good for her. As she rides, her mind wanders, slipping into a trance-like state as her body goes on automatic pilot.

She's spending more time with Tim and enjoying the easy feeling of being with him. She's learned more about him. He's a talented photographer and runs his freelance business, but he also works full time with a professional theatre company.

"That's why you're home during the day!"

He nods.

"I used to feel sorry for you. I thought you were out of work, but you never seemed very worried about it."

"Nope. Lots of work, as it happens."

"Is the set designing just filling in until you get starring roles?"

"Never! Never wanted to do that. I work backstage. Actually, I do some of the costumes, too — designing them, not making them. In between times, I'm the assistant stage manager. That means you have all the fun of a production but you don't have to memorize lines. You can read your cues and create magic."

As the months wind by, they become closer friends. It's comfortable not to have to worry about the boy-girl thing. Looking at Tim, adding up his artistic talents, his tea-drinking, and his gentle personality, she realizes he's gay. And that means safe.

While her friendship with Tim ripens, Al continues to call. He's coming over this evening because there's something else that he "needs" to talk to her about. She's suspicious about what's happening. He behaves as though they're in dating mode. They're not. At least, she's not. Is he looking for a replacement for his girlfriend? Is he tired of looking after himself? If he's genuinely interested in reconciliation, that's too bad, because she isn't. It's flattering, of course, to be wooed by an ex, but it's also dangerous ground to walk on. Her head knows they're divorced, but her body doesn't. There's a set of perfidious responses, learned over the long years together, that kick in of their own accord.

She invites him for dinner, hoping she can end the evening more quickly that way. She does a casserole of veggies, chicken, and rice. Served with crusty bread, it's easy but elegant, or at least, elegant enough. She doesn't have to impress Al. She doesn't have to impress anybody. She doesn't even have to impress *herself* anymore. She knows she can use up every pot in the kitchen if she wants to, and bring off a wall-to-wall cooking effort. But she doesn't have to. There's a wonderful freedom in that.

The casserole is in the oven, the table is set, and the apartment is as tidy as she feels like making it. That means clean towels in the bathroom, but she's not into candles and linen napkins.

Al arrives with an unexpected bouquet of flowers.

"Uh — thank you." She hates herself for stammering. "They're lovely."

They are, but she wishes he hadn't brought them, and tells him so.

"I know, Babe, but I couldn't resist them. They reminded me of you."

And the ball bounces back into Ellen's court. She's said the wrong thing. Again. Instead of telling him he didn't have to bring flowers, she should have told him she didn't want him to bring flowers. There's a difference.

Maybe, she thinks, *if we'd been more open with each other and communicated better, things might have been different.*

No, she decides. The problem had more to do with honesty than communication. She was too afraid of provoking his anger to tell him what she really thought, meant, or wanted.

This business with the flowers is typical, she tells herself. What she *means* is, "I don't want you to do that because I really don't want flowers from you," But what he *hears* is "My, that was nice of you. I'll say you didn't have to do it because that's the polite thing to do, but the truth is, I'm awfully glad you did."

That isn't the message she wants to send.

If he backhanded her around the room, there wouldn't be a problem. She'd throw him out and get a restraining order or lay assault charges. But how does she protest against insidious kindness? Kindness that violates her space? It's a type of abuse and she's an accomplice because she's letting it happen.

Helplessly, she waves the flowers around, then puts them on the kitchen counter.

"I don't have a vase," she tells him.

"That doesn't matter," he replies. "Just seeing the pleasure on your face when you saw them is enough. I'll bring you a vase the next time I come over. I've got lots."

Indeed. She knows exactly which vases he's talking about. There are at least a dozen in the cupboard at home — their house, no, *his* house. Vases that were gifts over the years, vases she'd bought at funny little shops and at flea markets.

She doesn't want them here. She doesn't want them anywhere. They're no longer part of her life.

Her mind suddenly registers his words: *Next time.* Nice and easy and familiar, like there's no doubt there will be a next time, a lot of next times. Even while her mind roils, her lips form the automatic response: "Thank you."

She takes a plastic jug from the cupboard and angrily jams the flowers into it.

"That'll do for now," she says. "You can take them with you when you leave."

She pulls the casserole from the oven and they seat themselves at the table. While he eats, his eyes roam around the apartment.

"Nice place you've got here," he says.

She makes a polite noise.

He looks around some more, then a grin splits his face.

"Okay," he laughs. "What's with the bike? Looks like a good one."

"It is," she agrees. "That's what I've been doing lately. Riding."

He looks at her approvingly. "So that's it. You look in awfully good shape. I mean, the shape has always been good, but you look in good condition, too." He laughs at his own joke.

She ignores it.

"I try to ride most days. It's harder during the rainy season, but I manage. And it's wonderful during the nice weather."

"Where do you ride?"

"Oh, just around."

"Maybe I could come with you sometime."

She lets that pass. Once again, she's made the wrong move. He takes her silence for agreement.

"If you're going out this weekend, I'll come over and we can start from here."

He busies himself eating for a few minutes while she says nothing, shoving veggies around on her plate, arranging carrots in straight lines and kernels of corn in gentle curlicues.

"Actually, it's supposed to be nice this weekend," he resumes. "What time do you go?"

"Oh, it varies," she says, weakly.

Way to go Ellen! That's the old backbone. That's letting him know you don't want him to intrude on your ride.

Not surprisingly, he doesn't recognize her comment for what she means it to be. Even she can't recognize it as what she wants to say. She changes the subject.

"What was it you wanted to talk about?"

He finishes his mouthful, puts the fork down, and sits up straight in his chair. It's his Chairman of the Board stance.

"I've been looking around the place lately, and there's an awful lot of stuff that we don't really need to keep. Like, things the kids left when they moved out. I know we told them they could store it there for a while, but they all have places of their own now and it's time they dealt with things like grownups. So I'm going to tell them they have to decide what they really want to keep, want enough to take into their own homes, and we can get rid of the rest.

"The girls still have their old doll house in the rec room. Even their bedroom is the same as it always was. We need to think about redoing the house, do some updating. And it needs painting, that sort of thing. I need to know if there's anything you want. I hoped you'd help me go through some of the boxes — the family pictures, the old home movies — do we want any of them? Should we get them converted to DVD? That sort of thing."

She wonders how much of this is his own thinking and how much is left over from the Bimbo ... sorry, *Verna*. Ellen can almost hear Verna's squeaky voice as she tracks around the house, complaining about the residue from Al's family. Reminders of the past. Intrusions on her turf.

She tries to ignore the number of times he said "we" in that statement, then realizes he's waiting for acquiescence.

"I guess there is a lot of clutter," she agrees. "Are you thinking of selling the house? Is that what's prompting this? Or is it any of my business?"

"Hey, Ellie. It's always your business. You're entitled to know. I mean, it was your home too for a lot of years. It could still be your home if you wanted."

"No, Al. It couldn't. We're not in that space anymore. Remember?"

He laughs. "Can't blame a guy for trying."

He sounds like too many late night movies. Ellen's sure she's heard this dialogue before, with and without violins. So far everything he's said has been a cliché. It rolls so smoothly from his lips she wonders if he rehearses his lines while he shaves in the morning, practising the expressions that go with them.

"So, are you planning to sell?"

"No, nothing that drastic. At least, not right now. The bottom line is, the place looks a little tired and I didn't want to do anything without talking to you. Maybe you could come over and take a look? Give me an idea of what's worth keeping — or what needs doing."

"Al, I keep telling you, do what you want with the house. Fix it up however you want. You wouldn't be comfortable with my suggestions."

"Not true, Babe. We may have had our disagreements, but I always thought you had great taste. Still do. I'd value your suggestions. And I don't want to get rid of anything you might want. That's only fair, isn't it?"

She thinks about it.

"So, when do you plan to do all this?"

"No timeline. Just whenever it's convenient for you. How'd it be if we went for a little ride this weekend, then we could go back to the house and check out a few things? I could maybe put together a little dinner for us. Does that sound like a good idea?"

It sounds like a crappy idea, but her head nods up and down in agreement, like the bobble-headed toys in the back window of teenagers' cars. What she needs is a neck brace to prevent herself from agreeing to things she doesn't want to do. And this is definitely something she doesn't want to do. But it's hard to turn down a request that sounds so reasonable.

"Okay," she says. "But let's skip the ride. I'll come over after lunch."

The evening dribbles on. They chat about nothing in particular. He settles in, she tries to bring the evening to a close. He starts to clear away the dishes.

"I'd really rather you didn't," she tells him. "It's a small kitchen and you don't know where things go. It'll only take me a minute to clear up after you leave."

There. She's finally said the magic word: *Leave*. But he's got his blinders on. Selective hearing. He dials her out. Instead of picking up on the real message — "It's time for you to go" — he hears only, "We'll spend our time together doing something more interesting than dishes."

"You know, I'd almost forgotten what a good cook you are. That was a terrific dinner, Ellie."

Now that's a piece of crap. Ellie's not a good cook. She never was and never will be. She doesn't have the patience, or the imagination. She can produce a fancy meal but it doesn't come easily. Over the years she tailored her cooking to his tastes. That's more than likely what he's referring to. Bimbo didn't have enough time to learn all his likes and dislikes, so she couldn't score very high marks in that field.

She smiles to herself, imagining exactly where Verna did score high marks and wondering what happened to wipe them out. Al knew she wasn't Ellen when he first started going out with her. That's *why* he started going out with her. Now he keeps repeating "She wasn't you, Babe," every time Verna's name comes up, as though it caught him by surprise.

He notices her sudden smile, takes it as gratitude for his comment on her cooking, and continues to talk. Words drift aimlessly between them, like softballs in a sandlot. He tosses a pitch. She bunts. It isn't a conversation. They're just making noises — Al because he doesn't want to go, Ellen because she doesn't want him to stay. Finally he looks at his watch and makes a face that tries to indicate surprise.

"My gosh! I didn't realize it was this late. I didn't mean to stay this long. Sure I can't help with those dishes before I go?"

She shakes her head. Then the shuffling begins. He gets his jacket from the hall, she takes the flowers from the jug, holds them over the sink, shaking the water from the stems, and stuffs them into a plastic bag.

"Hey, Babe, I really wanted you to have those flowers."

She's flustered again. She really doesn't want them. In her minimal lifestyle, juice is a more useful commodity than flowers and she needs the jug to make juice in the morning.

He puts his arm around her, takes the flowers from her hand, and puts them back on the counter.

"Come on, Babe. Bend a little. It won't hurt you to take a few flowers. We can at least be friends, can't we?"

Ellen knows the expected response: of course they can be friends. But she's not sure at this moment if the expected response is the safe response. She says nothing. But it's the most dangerous response of all, because it lets him assume what he wants to hear. He closes his arms around her and gives her a hug.

"Okay, Babe. Thanks for the dinner, and for the evening. I enjoyed them both. I'll see you on Saturday — my treat this time. You'll be surprised at what I've learned in the kitchen."

He pauses, grinning. It sounds like an invitation to play straight man in some shticky routine he's figured out. She doesn't want to play. She doesn't care what he's learned in the kitchen. Or any other room in the house. Or who he learned them from. But she doesn't say any of this.

"Okay, Al. I'll see you Saturday and we can look at whatever needs to be done."

She finally eases him out, evading another attempt at a hug. As the door clicks shut, she retraces her steps, picks up the flowers, and jams them in the garbage. She really does need the jug.

That night she has trouble getting to sleep.

"What kind of spineless nit are you?" she berates herself. "Why didn't you just tell him to burn the house down if he really wants to get rid of all the stuff that's in it? You're dumb, you know that?"

Lying motionless in bed, watching shadows move in the dark, she realizes she's backing herself into a corner. It's a lose-lose situation. At this moment, she doesn't know how to get out of it, and that really scares her.

※

The rest of the week plods by.

She wakens early on Saturday. The sky is clear.

"To hell with you, Al," she fumes, as she chokes down a quick breakfast. "You don't have any right to come waltzing in and upset my life like this."

The bike flaunts its gleaming chrome handlebars, shooting sparkling reflections around the room. It's an inanimate object, so why is it laughing at her, spraying sunbeams around like that? The tree branch outside her window waves.

"That's odd," she says. "There isn't any wind."

The motion is explained when a small bird suddenly hops into view, bounces cheekily along the branch, and pauses, cocking its head to one side and regarding Ellen for a long minute. She freezes. The lack of motion reassures him and he resumes his cheerful path along the branch. Suddenly he throws back his head and begins to sing. The song is out of all proportion to his size. How can a drab black and brown bird, hardly larger than her thumb, contain a song of such proportions? On and on he goes, secure in his environment, affirming his universe. Ellen presses closer to the window. The motion catches his eye and he stops, instantly, leftover bits of song hanging in the air. He peers intently in her direction. She freezes, but he isn't so easily fooled this time. With a quick motion he launches himself through the branches and soars away.

She moves to the window, looking in all directions, but he's gone. She feels bereft, as though someone has taken something from her.

"I wish I could disappear like that," she whispers. Sighing, she turns from the window. Once again, the bike presents itself. There's a subtle invitation: "Let's ride. Just us. Let's go. Anywhere you want."

Ruefully she shakes her head. "Don't I wish. But I can't. I just can't."

Suddenly she hears the birdsong again. Why is everything free but her? A voice inside her head turns her words around ad throws them back: Why is she not free? Ellen repeats the question to herself. Why not?

"Damn it, he has no control over me."

Angrily she heads for the bedroom, pulls on her riding gear, and stomps into the kitchen to fill a water bottle.

"I *am* free. He has no right to say what I can or can't do. Blast you anyway, Al," she rants, buckling on her fanny pack. "You don't have any right to mess up my life like this. I can go riding if I want to. And if I'm late getting back, that's just too darn bad. And if it wrecks your lunch, I don't care."

Ellen grabs her bike, backs out of the apartment, and lets the door slam shut behind her. She's still muttering as she reaches the lobby and wheels the bike out of the elevator. She leans the bike against her hip as she buckles on her helmet, pulls on her gloves, and tightens the Velcro closures. She doesn't realize anyone else is in the lobby until she moves toward the door and a hand slides into her field of vision.

"Here, let me get that for you," a man says, a small smile quirking his lips.

Startled, she looks at him blankly. She doesn't recognize him. He must be one of the other tenants.

"Uh, thank you."

Brilliant conversation. Simply sparkling. How could he ever forget an exchange like that? On the other hand, does she care if he remembers her?

She looks again. The smile is still there — a warm sort of smile. Almost friendly. He isn't laughing at her, he's laughing *with* her.

"It's okay," he says. "I get days like that, too. You'll probably feel better when you finish your ride."

He brings the conversation to an end, releasing the door so it drifts shut between them. He does it pleasantly, with a smile and a little wave of the hand from the other side of the glass. He doesn't stand and watch. She's free to go.

The whirr of tires and the soft spinning sound of the chain smoothes away her mental carbuncles. There's a little bit of a breeze now, nothing heavy, but a hint of cooler days to come. She won't be able to do this much longer.

"Enjoy it while you can," she mutters.

The texture of the road changes and her tires alter their sound to match. Ellen's learned a vocabulary of road sounds. Each type of pavement makes its own distinctive music. The road along the top of the dike is compacted gravel that makes a shushing sound. There are a couple of sandy patches that whisper as the bike passes by, flinging tiny pieces of grit against her fender. It's different from the *tink tink* of small pieces of gravel rattling against it. Asphalt has a soft sound to it, while cement makes a rigid noise.

Ellen tries to ride around things when she can. There's a lot of glass on the road. Here and there, ominous piles mark the site of an accident. A pile of red glass is a brake light. Clear, ribbed glass from a headlight marks another collision. Small, green-tinged cubes of safety glass from a window bespeak a more serious encounter. Once in a while there are corroborating pieces of metal and plastic nearby, crumpled bits of chrome, twisted blades from windshield wipers. There's an ongoing story in the things that lie beside the road. They keep her mind occupied for long stretches of time.

Today, though, Ellen isn't in the mood for reading the road. She's tuning in to herself, listening deep inside, trying to envision what might happen this afternoon. What she will do. What he will do. Maybe, she tells herself, maybe if she thinks it through beforehand, if she finds the pitfalls, she can protect herself, rather than being caught by surprise and leaving herself vulnerable.

Somehow, she seems always to be at risk as far as Al is concerned, as far as anyone is concerned. This time, she vows, she'll be ready for whatever goofy shots he lobs at her.

When she finally turns her wheels homeward she feels at peace, her mind calm and settled and the afternoon no longer a threat.

— 11 —

ELLEN FINDS SOMETHING UNSETTLING in coming back to the place she once lived. The house is familiar, but strange in a way she can't define.

Al must have been lurking on the other side of the door as she walked up the steps. He catapults across the threshold like an exuberant puppy.

"Babe! You're here! It's great to see you again." He burbles on, making welcome host noises. "You caught me by surprise. I didn't hear the car."

"I didn't drive. I took the bus," she replies, shrugging out of her coat. A small scuffle ensues as he tries to grab the coat and put it in the hall closet. She does, after all, know where the closet is. She's hung hundreds of coats in it, including this one.

"No, here. Let me take that," he insists, out-positioning her with a coat hanger. He turns his mind to her first comment.

"How come you took the bus? Problems with the car?"

She shakes her head. "Nope. No problems." Damned if she'll confess that she doesn't have the money for insurance. "I've been trying to use alternate transportation lately. You know, pollution and all that."

He isn't buying it. Not for a minute. His eyes are a pair of little computer screens that mirror the thoughts passing behind them. There's a full stop as he decides whether to pursue this or not. Discretion wins. He's concerned enough about getting the visit off to a good start that he'll put up with whatever she says.

He turns away and fusses with the coat. It's not such a difficult thing to do, really. Just shove one end of the hanger in each of the arms, turn around and drop the hook over the rod in the closet. Somehow the familiar action seems foreign to him, like he's never done it before, or like he's being judged on his performance. Should she award a 7.2? Or has it been a 9.5?

She scolds herself. *Stop it. The guy's trying. You're going to end up making some smart-assed comment and setting off an argument that will, at the very least, throw him into some completely counter-productive, full frontal sulks.*

The coat is finally hung and he turns back to her, cupping her elbow in his hand and steering her down the hall, the hall she's walked ten thousand times before. In daylight. In darkness. With him. With kids. With friends. By herself. She tries to extricate her elbow, but he isn't letting go.

"Here, let's sit in the front room." He propels her through the archway before releasing his hold.

Her eyes skim the room, looking for changes. There are a couple of empty spaces where there used to be photographs that included her, other blanks that once held keepsakes.

"I didn't change anything, Ellie," he says, morphing his eyes into cocker-spaniel mode. "I couldn't."

She doesn't know how to respond. There's nothing to be gained by pointing out the missing pictures or small treasures. She drops her eyes to her lap, examining her hands, demurely folded in front of her. The white line where her wedding ring used to be has disappeared, but the indentation is still there. She wonders how long that takes to go away, or if it ever does. Is this the stigmata of divorce? Deep grooves that can't be excised?

Al waits for a comment. She obliges.

"So, where do you want to start? In the kids' rooms? The basement?"

His eyes snap back to normal. "Oh, yeah. I thought maybe we could have a bit of lunch first and then start with the girls' room, if that's okay with you."

"Sure. Doesn't matter to me."

Back to you, she thinks. Serve, lob, return. Your point, her point. But no love.

A small scowl drifts across his face. Obviously she's lost her place in the script he's prepared for them. Time to regroup. He stands, quickly.

"Hope you don't mind eating in the kitchen. It seems more … informal."

Ellen almost laughs out loud.

"By all means, let's not get formal. That just leaves you with a sink full of dishes, a stack of napkins to wash, and a tablecloth to iron. And I don't imagine you're any fonder of ironing than I am."

She invites him to share the joke.

"I wouldn't mind, Babe, if that's what you want," he says earnestly.

She's in serious danger of barfing.

"No, not at all. Kitchen sounds fine to me. Something smells good. Am I witnessing your debut as a chef?"

Now it's his turn to be flustered.

"Nothing that grand. Most of it's from the frozen food section. They've got great stuff there, you know? All I had to do was bring it home and stuff it in the oven."

"So what do I smell?"

"Chicken pot pies. The good ones. Not as good as the ones you used to make, of course, but pretty good."

She nods. "I haven't made one for ages. It really isn't worthwhile for one person. Or two," she adds, hastily.

The kitchen table is set with a bright pair of placemats she hasn't seen before. There's a jug of flowers in the middle of the table — small, low flowers, placed in one of her old cream jugs that lost its sugar-bowl years ago but was too good to throw out.

"That's an interesting idea," she says, gesturing toward the table. "I never could figure out what to do with the jug. I should have thrown it out years ago."

He smiles. "Yeah, well, I'm glad you didn't."

He's happy to take credit, but Ellen's willing to bet the whole set of china that it wasn't his idea. Nor were the placemats. It's the first positive trace she's seen of the Bimbo. Glancing around the kitchen she spots a couple of other items she's sure also originated with the girlfriend. She doesn't comment on them.

Al bustles around the stove as she seats herself at the table. He pulls out a pair of nicely browned chicken pies. And he's wearing new oven mitts. She'll give him the benefit of the doubt on that one. Doing his own laundry may have made him realize that the stuff that bubbles out of pies and casseroles stains towels and that's why you use oven mitts. Unlikely, but possible. However, he uses an oven witch to pull the rack out — a hooked stick, this one in the shape of a flying duck, that lets you pull the rack out without burning your wrists on the hot oven. Ellen knows he'd *never* buy that, ergo it's left over from Bimbo. Not that it's any of her business, she tells herself.

He puts the pies on a trivet that sits in the middle of the stove. Things have really changed around here. He turns to the fridge and whips out a salad, neatly covered with a tight film of plastic wrap. The toaster oven yields some crusty buns.

"I'm impressed, Al," she tells him. "This looks great."

He basks in her approval.

Lunch is awkward. Small talk comes hard to both of them. Eventually they finish and she begins to stack the dishes.

"Oh, no. Leave them. I'll get them later," he says.

"I can at least help clear the table," she insists, but he reaches out to take the stack from her. They're back to their formal pas de deux. She shrugs, grins, and moves away.

"Okay, what's first on the agenda?"

They look at the twins' room. It isn't too bad. The girls dealt with most of their possessions, but when they move on to the boys rooms, she realizes they are virtually untouched — posters on the walls, airplane models hanging from the ceiling, even drawers full of outgrown jeans and sweaters.

"Remember this?" Al says, holding up Geoff's old hockey sweater. "How many hours did we spend at the rink with that kid?"

Everything has a *remember* attached and Al's determined to trot them all out. She suspects it's going to be a long afternoon.

It is. It drags endlessly on as Al examines the minutia and trivia of Geoff's life. Eventually they move to Robby's room, where the process repeats itself as the afternoon wanes.

Finally, it's time to snap on the light.

"Gosh, I had no idea it was that late. And we haven't got near the rec room or the basement. Now that we're on a roll, how'd it be if I order something in and we can just keep going?"

Ellen decides lying is the easiest way out.

"Gosh, I'm sorry," she says, looking at her watch. "But I really have to go." She scrambles to her feet and looks around the room. "Well, at least we got some of it done. You can call one of the charities and they'll come and pick up the shoes and clothing. The boys can decide what to do with the rest of it."

Getting out of the house is like broken field running as she dodges one block after another: No, she doesn't want a drink. No, she doesn't want to take the photograph albums. No, she doesn't want a ride home.

She surreptitiously checks the schedule in her pocket. The bus is due in a few minutes. It arrives on cue and whisks her away. Ellen glances out the window and sees Al, still standing on the porch. She expects the Bimbo to bounce out from around the corner. Has she really gone, or was she just hiding in the basement?

❋

Walking into the vestibule of her building, Ellen sees a friendly face. Tim smiles and nods a greeting. "You're out late," he says. Even in the dim light she can see the sparkle in his eyes.

"Yes, I've been out visiting …" She pauses. "Just an old friend," she says, finally.

"Lucky you. There's no friends like old friends. My old friends are all living somewhere else. I wish I could hop on a bus and see them."

"Where would that be, Tim? All the time we've known each other, you've never told me where you're from."

"Why, Ireland, of course!"

She's surprised. He doesn't sound Irish. She tells him so.

He's pleased. "It took a lot of effort on my part to lose that accent."

"Why would you do that?"

"It limits the things I can do."

How strange. What difference would an accent make for a photographer?

"Have you been in this country very long?" she asks.

He pauses before answering.

"Aye. It's been a long while now. And too long since I've been home."

"How long is too long?"

"Persistent, aren't you?" he quips. "All right then, I'll give you an exact answer. It's been fourteen years and seven days."

"That's pretty precise. How can you know that exactly?"

"Not difficult at all. I left home on my birthday, fourteen years ago. My birthday was exactly one week ago."

"I'm sorry; I didn't know your birthday was last week. Many happy returns."

"Ah, that's not good enough. In a civilized country, a man gets a kiss on his birthday."

He smiles, expectantly, and she salutes his birthday with a friendly peck on the cheek. Laughing, they enter the elevator.

— 12 —

SUMMER IS COMING TO an end. Neighbourhood lawns show patches of brown. Flowers, once lush and vigorous, wilt in on themselves, their brilliant colours faded by the sun. Hedges stand docile within their sculptured outlines. The gardens are waiting. Even the birds are muted, their morning-song no longer fresh and challenging. They sound like faded road signs, mere formalities standing by the highway.

Ellen stores up pleasure in her rides, like a squirrel greedily hiding tidbits for the long, dreary months ahead. When the rains begin, there will be few opportunities to ride. The very thought is depressing.

Al invites himself to ride with her on Saturday. She plans a sixty-kilometre trip along the river and out into the countryside. It's a beautiful ride. There's always something to watch on the river and the road has some nice changes: dead level at times, it shifts to rolling hills with a couple of gut-buster climbs. Good ones. Steep enough to be a real challenge but short enough to be achieved.

"I'm leaving at seven in the morning," she warns Al. "Traffic is light then and with an early start we can make a couple of stops if we have to."

"You won't have to stop on my account, Babe," he replies.

Her gear is ready: a nylon shell to put over her jersey in case of rain — an unlikely prospect given the weather forecast, but a precaution she's learned to take. Both water bottles are full, one with clear water, the other with an energizing sport drink. Her pump is hooked firmly in place under the top bar of the frame. The little pouch under her seat holds a tool kit, a spare tube, an old one-dollar bill to put across a puncture, a credit card for emergencies, personal identification, a power gel, and an orange. There's just enough room to squeeze in her key chain.

The buzzer snarls out Al's "shave and a hair-cut" entry signal.

"Hi," she calls, leaning toward the intercom on the wall. "Are you coming up?"

His voice warps through the buzzes and crackles of the speaker. Remote. Alien-sounding. "No. I'll wait here."

"Okay. I'll be right down."

Time for one last visit to the bathroom. She's getting canny at finding bathrooms along the road, but a pit stop is always the last thing before leaving home. Earlier trips were agonizing. She used to feel compelled to order endless cups of coffee that she didn't drink, simply to entitle her to use facilities in the fast food places that dot the highways. Now she's less self-conscious. Gas station attendants are miserable about giving their precious washroom keys to cyclists. Ellen points out that she is *also* a driver whose product loyalty can easily be swayed to a competing station that is more gracious in sharing facilities. Desperation turns her brazen.

Al greets her with an appreciative whistle and, despite herself, she starts to laugh. In the early days of their marriage, when watching late night movies on TV was their only affordable entertainment, the wolf whistle turned up in shows from the forties. Probably no one under fifty has ever heard an actual wolf whistle today.

"I'd forgotten what a trim figure you used to have," he says. "Still do," he adds, rolling his eyes like Groucho Marx and flicking an imaginary cigar. "Let's strike a medal for the man who invented Spandex."

"Oh, hush," she says, praying that the warmth that floods her cheeks won't turn into a full-scale blush. She's too old for that. She casts about for a way to change the subject.

From somewhere, he's gotten a helmet. It might even be an old one of Rob's. The tires on his bike have the deep, rich, black rubber look that says they're brand new. The tread isn't scuffed yet and the sidewalls still prickle with little stubs of rubber from the mould. He's wearing shorts and a T-shirt. No jacket in sight. There's a bag laced onto the rat-trap carrier on the back that looks like it holds enough groceries for a Scout troop picnic. He doesn't have a water bottle. That concerns her.

"Can I loan you a water bottle?" she asks.

His look is pure derision. "Nah, I won't need it. I've got a couple of cans of pop in my lunch."

"Okay, then. Let's go."

Confidently, she straddles her bike and pushes off. With a rush, Al pulls ahead of her and turns left out of the driveway.

"Hey, where are you going? I thought we'd agreed to head up the river? We need to go the other way for that."

He swings around in a slow circle.

"It's too far. I thought we'd just go for a short ride. Maybe go along the bike trail to the bridge and cut over."

She stops, dismounts, and resets the bike on its kickstand.

"Wait a minute. We agreed on this. You never mentioned that route."

"Yeah, but I've been thinking about it. The river is too far. And there's some nice places near the bridge for a picnic."

She chokes back a rude retort.

"Al, if you want to go on a picnic, I'll go on a picnic with you. But not today. Today I'm going to ride. If you want to come with me, that's great. But I'm not changing my plans."

"Okay. We'll picnic another day. The river it is."

Her knees go weak but her hands relax. A deep breath helps

control the buzzing in her head and the tightness in her chest. Something has happened. Something strange. She's not sure if she's ready for it.

"You're sure you can make it?" she asks.

"No problem. If you can do it, I can do it."

"Look, you don't have to be a hero. If you get tired, sing out and we can take a break, okay?"

He grins in response.

She has a choice. She can either ride him into the ground — and she knows she can do that — or call the stops herself. She knows how stubborn he is. And how intensely competitive in everything he does. He has to hike farther, walk faster, carry a bigger load, and work longer hours than anyone else. His theme song should be that old chestnut from *Annie Get Your Gun* — "Anything You Can Do, I Can Do Better."

"Okay. Let's go." She pushes off, keeping an eye on him in her rear-view mirror.

Labour Day weekend is over, but cars and vans with families head out for a last weekend at the cottage, last trip to the beach, last run with the boat. Shopping mall parking lots are crowded with kids buying school supplies and back-to-school wear.

When Ellen's kids were in school, they, like everyone else, went to school on the first day to register, then rushed home at noon with a supply list. Ellen would join the afternoon stampede through the mall stores as everyone tried to get everything on the same day. Long lines of frantic parents, small kids screaming from fatigue, cranky clerks trying to cope with the surging tide of shoppers. It was worse than Christmas shopping. There is no goodwill or friendly trappings of the season, just grim adults and sullen children trying to get through a ritual that stressed both patience and budgets.

Minor arguments rumbled along like movie soundtracks.

"You don't need a new (loose leaf binder, box of crayons, gym shorts, etc.) Last year's is still good."

"These are different. Miss (Whoever) says we have to get this kind."

"Well, I don't see why. The others are perfectly good."

"Everyone else will have the right ones and I'll have the wrong kind."

Abruptly, Ellen swings back to the present and realizes she's ignoring Al. Quickly, she checks her rear-view mirror. He's plugging along, but dropping behind. She slows her pace and waits for him to catch up. Reluctantly, she slows even more and watches him edge closer. No matter what she said earlier, she knows now the ride will be much shorter and much easier than what she had planned — the ride Al had agreed to when they talked about it earlier.

Eventually he pulls up even with her.

"What's up? Got a problem?"

"Nope. Just decided to wait for you. The road's wide enough to ride beside each other here. Unless you'd rather ride by yourself."

He shakes his head. The helmet wobbles. It needs adjusting. She wonders how to suggest it without stirring his anger.

"Don't matter to me. There's a pretty good view from back here." He grins, wickedly. It takes her back to a hundred tender moments. Moments when they were much gentler with each other. Moments when their lives focused on each other.

"I'll ignore that," she tells him. "If you behave yourself, you can ride beside me. If you don't, I might even make you ride in front. Then we'll see about the view."

"You might even enjoy it," he quips.

"Oh, please! Let's not shovel all that modesty around. It clogs the treads on my tires."

They laugh. It's repartee the likes of which they've shared countless times, a bridge to a familiar past. The road whirrs by under their tires. A bypass looms ahead.

"The road narrows here. Want me to go ahead?"

He nods, head down and breathing a little harder. They turn off to the right, fly down the bypass, across a level stretch, and rejoin the highway. Just ahead is Samson's, a store that's grown from a ramshackle fish and bait shop to a good-sized store with groceries, delicatessen, arts, crafts, giftware, and an extensive seafood counter. They pull in and dismount. Ellen makes a show of checking her tires. No surprises. They're fine, just as she knew they would be.

"Want me to throw the gauge on yours?" she asks. The silver stick reflects the sun.

"Nah. They're okay," he says, shoving his thumb against a sidewall.

"Feel like a bit of a break?"

"Only if you do."

That means yes, but he doesn't want to say so.

"I usually stop here for a cold drink," she tells him. She doesn't add that she usually stops for the cold drink on the way home at the end of a long ride. "They've got some great juices. Why don't you watch the bikes and I'll get something for both of us?"

He lowers himself to the curb.

"Sounds good to me."

Ellen chooses a bottle of apple juice, picks up a paper cup from the deli, and pays for her purchase. Through the window, she sees him relaxing in the sunshine.

She walks outside, pours a mouthful of juice into the cup, then passes the bottle to him. They sit in silence, sipping their drinks, watching the traffic drone by.

"You know, it's been a long time since I've done anything like this," he says, at last.

"If you're tired, we can go back."

"No, I didn't mean it that way. I just meant it's been a long time since I've done anything this much fun. Makes me feel like a kid again. No appointments, no hassles. It's great."

His hand engulfs hers.

"I can see why you like it. We should have done this years ago."

Ellen says nothing. After a moment, he gives her hand another squeeze, then releases it.

"Well, I guess we better get going before I stiffen up."

She picks up the litter, deposits the bottle in a recycling rack and the cup in a trash barrel, then they straddle their bikes again and push off.

The ride lasts much longer than she had expected, even allowing for Al's inexperience. They make many stops. Still, she has to give him *A* for effort. As long as she remembers to slow her pace, he tries hard to keep up. There's no point in running him ragged. They have to complete the circuit to get back home. She keeps a careful eye on him and enjoys a nice, easy ride.

During the early part of the ride, they exchange trivial comments, but by the end of the day they're actually exchanging ideas and discussing things. She disagrees with him on some things and explains why. He listens and considers what she's said, instead of rejecting it out of hand.

"You know, you might be right. I've never thought about it that way."

It's a wide divergence from what their conversations had become toward the end of their marriage — or their non-conversations, that is, when it didn't seem worthwhile to even try discussing anything.

At last the ride ends and they pull into the parking area at Ellen's apartment block. There's a long pause. His body language is loud and clear. He doesn't want to leave yet. She asks him up.

"Come on. I'll make us something to eat and you can have a bit of a rest before you head home."

"Sounds good to me, Babe."

She opens the door and he wheels his bike in.

"You can leave yours in the lobby," she says, as the elevator door opens and she walks her bike in, tipping it upright.

"I hadn't planned on dinner," she tells him, as they rumble upward, "but I've got the makings for some spaghetti, if that's okay."

"At this moment, anything would be okay."

As they enter the apartment, she heads for the bedroom. "I'm just going to skin out of these clothes. I'll only be a minute. Sit down and make yourself comfortable."

He waves his hand. "Hey, take your time. Take a shower if you want. I'll be quite happy to sit here for a bit without having to pedal."

"Okay. I'll take you up on that."

She sets some kind of record for quick showering, dries off, slips into baggy sweats and a loose shirt, and towels her hair dry as she comes back into the living room.

"Listen, I don't have anything for you to change into, but if you want to have a bit of a wash, there's lots of time before we eat."

He starts to reject the suggestion, then reconsiders.

"You know, that would feel great."

She hands him a clean towel and he heads into the bathroom while she scurries around the tiny kitchen, organizing ingredients for dinner. There's no wine, but there is juice. For a potluck supper, it'll have to do.

Minutes later, Al steps out of the bathroom, bare-chested, with the towel wrapped around his waist. He holds a soggy pile of clothing in one hand.

"Babe, I'm sorry about this. I was just going to wash in the basin but the shower looked so inviting I thought I'd have a quick one and hop back into my clothes, but when I went to put them on I discovered I hadn't pulled the curtain all the way closed and my clothes are soaked. Do you have a dryer I could throw them in?"

He reminds her of Robby and Geoff as little kids, when they were stuck with some kind of mess to clean up. His eyes are their eyes, his expression their expressions.

"No problem." She takes the clothing from his hands. "I'll just toss these into the washer before I dry them — then you'll have something clean to wear home. That is, if you don't mind dining like that?"

"Actually, this towel is wet too. Do you have a dry one?"

Ellen giggles. "You're in luck. I do have another dry towel — a large, dry towel."

His expression of relief provokes another ripple of laughter.

"Thanks, Babe."

Moments later, his clothing is churning around in the washer along with a wet towel and he's kilted in a dry towel topped by an outsized sweatshirt she sometimes wears as a nightshirt. The effect is raffish, but at least he's clean and dry. And in a good mood.

They share laughter with their dinner, toasting the ride with twin cans of root beer.

"That was great," Al says, helping to clear the dishes from the table. "Actually, the whole day was wonderful. Not what I expected. You surprised me. I didn't think you'd be able to ride that far. You did great. You really did."

"So did you. Maybe we shouldn't have gone quite that far, but you were a good sport. I enjoyed it too."

Abruptly, the washer stops and she jumps up.

"Your clothes. I'll toss them in the dryer. They won't take long."

"Actually, they should take about forty minutes," he says. "Jeans are harder to dry, but the shirt will dry quickly."

Ellen looks at him blankly.

"Who do you think does my laundry?" he asks. "I've learned a whole lot about it lately. I know exactly how long it takes to dry a load, so I know we have about forty minutes to get the kitchen cleaned up. I'll help with the dishes. You might not believe it, but these days I'm a pretty good hand with a dishwasher, dish-cloth, or a dish towel."

Once the kitchen is tidy, they sit enveloped in an easy com-panionship. Talk flows seamlessly. Too soon, the timer rings, announcing the end of the dryer cycle. There is a strange sense of *déjà vu* in taking his clothing from the dryer. Ellen folds it neatly, as she did a thousand times over the years, pressing the clothing against her body, feeling its warmth as she folds the jeans neatly, pairs his socks and cuffs them together, even though they are the only pair of socks in the load and he'll be putting them on in a few minutes.

She hands the stack of folded laundry to him, laughing at the sight of his toga-sarong. "You can change in the bedroom," she suggests, leading the way and opening the door.

He follows close behind. "Thanks, Babe. That was thought-ful. I guess you think I'm pretty dumb getting my stuff soaked like that."

"No, it was an accident. It could have happened to anyone."

"You know, that's one of the things I've missed since you've been gone. You're a nice person. Just genuinely nice." Awkwardly, he reaches out and grabs her hand.

"Oh, hell. I can't just keep holding your hand. Am I allowed to give you a hug? Just to say thank you?"

He moves closer, encompassing her in his arms. "Ah, Babe. I really have missed you. Today was wonderful. I hope we can do it again sometime."

Ellen snuggles into his shoulder and lets her arms slide across his back, enjoying the well-remembered feeling of his body against hers.

Slowly and gently, as though it was their first kiss, he slides one hand up over her shoulder, cupping his palm below her chin, tipping her face up to his. Sweetly and softly, his lips find hers. Without thinking, she finds herself responding. Then suddenly she feels a surge of heat as he pulls her closer, against the hard-muscled body she remembers so well.

A pulse, deep inside, begins to beat. Ellen moves her hand slowly over his back, drawing him closer. She feels something move and pulls back, startled.

"I think you dislodged my towel," he laughs. "My turn to dislodge something?"

He reaches toward her, slowly sliding the band of her sweat-pants past her hips. His hands are warm and compelling against her skin. The surge of passion that grips them both is so natural and so familiar. Ellen closes her eyes, ready to abandon herself to the lazy, languorous feeling that creeps through her body. It takes a minute to realize that the sudden interruption is her own voice calling out.

"Wait! Wait a minute!"

Shocked, he pulls back.

"What's wrong?"

"Nothing. Nothing's wrong. But I think it would be a good idea if you used this."

She reaches across to the top of the dresser, picking up a little square packet lying on a doily.

His eyes drop to her hand, then flick back to her face.

"You can't be serious."

"Oh, but I am."

"Come on, Ellie. You won't get pregnant."

"Probably not, but there are other things I can get."

"From me? Come off it. You know me better than that."

"Not necessarily from you, but from your girlfriend. Things aren't the same any more, Al. You've had at least one partner, and I'll bet any amount you want to name that she's had other partners as well. Probably quite a few. So, there's a lot more involved now than just you and me."

Silently he turns and begins putting on his clothes.

"Forget it. Just forget it. It was a lousy idea on my part."

Ellen shrugs. "Have it your own way. But if we're going to be involved with each other again — that way — then I have to think of myself. That means AIDS testing and condoms."

"You're serious, aren't you?"

Trying to control her shaking knees, she nods.

"Yes, Al, I am serious."

"I've never heard you talk like this. What's gotten into you?"

"Nothing," she says.

"Yeah. Right," he echoes. A grin flicks the corner of his mouth. "Sorry, that wasn't a good phrase to use, given the circumstances."

"Al, things have changed. I've learned to learn to look after myself. And I've learned to think for myself, as well."

Silence stretches between them, like a rubber band waiting to break. She tries hard to probe the currents he's sending out. Is he angry? Disgusted? She isn't sure where those unbidden words came from, or even where the idea came from. She'd never intended to use the condoms, never even thought of them. But suddenly she was grateful they were there.

He dresses and leaves quickly. After he goes, the apartment seems very empty, as though someone has drained it of some vital element.

Later that night, her bed seems endlessly wide, very large and very lonely. She wonders if she's suddenly gone crazy.

❋

Ellen feels comfortable sitting with Tim the next day, sharing their afternoon cup of tea. Her gay neighbour has become a true friend. She feels at ease with him and can talk to him about anything. They laugh a lot, about the same sorts of things.

"You're in a strange mood today," he says.

"Hmmm. I did a long ride yesterday."

"Ah, but you've done that before. And it doesn't seem like tiredness. More like you're at odds with yourself, or with someone else. I hope it isn't me?"

Ellen smiles and reaches for his hand. It's a nice hand. It accepts hers and offers just the right response to her squeeze.

"Can't hide things from you, can I, Tim? Are you psychic, or what?"

"People say the Irish are. Put it down to that if you want."

They sit for a moment, he expectantly, she trying to order her thoughts.

"You're right, Tim. There is something on my mind."

His eyebrows quirk into a question.

"I spent the day with my husband — my *ex*-husband. We went riding and I asked him up for dinner after."

"I see," he says, quietly. "Is this a reconciliation? Are you getting together again?"

"No. Nothing like that. At least, it didn't start out like that. I'm not even sure myself how it happened. Anyway, to make a long story short, he made a pass and I guess I was ready to go along with it. Then I asked him to use a condom."

Tim splutters into his teacup. "You what?"

Ellen grins. "Yeah, imagine. Me, who still blushes if anyone refers to them in public. I can't even believe I'm telling you this. It isn't the sort of thing I usually discuss, especially with a man."

"Well, you did with one man — yesterday."

"I did, didn't I? I still can't believe it."

"I'll bet he didn't believe it either."

She flushes. "He was a little upset."

"So what happened? Did you ask him if he had one?

"No, I couldn't have done that."

She pauses, remembering.

"There was a big promotion at the mall last week. A guy dressed like a doctor was wandering around the mall giving out samples. He handed me a few and wouldn't take them back. Said they were trying to teach kids about safe sex and would I please not send out a negative message by acting like they shouldn't be part of everyday life.

"I didn't want to be a bad sport, so I shoved them in my pocket and thought I'd get rid of them later. I put them on my dresser when I got home and forgot about them —until the moment came yesterday. That's when I remembered they were there, and handed him one."

Tim crows with laughter. "Oh, that's delightful! That's wonderful! I can just imagine the look on his face."

"Needless to say, it deflated the moment. Instantly."

"Did he stomp out?"

"No. He wasn't mad. It was more like, I don't know, like he was disillusioned or something. But it wasn't anger. I don't know what I expected."

The silence hangs for a moment, broken by the sound of Tim's spoon, moving slowly as a glob of honey dissolves in his cup.

"You must have surprised him," he says, finally.

"I'm sure I did."

"Look at it another way. He makes a pass and you seem receptive — and then you hand him a condom. There's a certain amount of premeditation to that. He must surely have wondered how you happened to have condoms lying so conveniently on top of your dresser. And whether you had occasion to use them frequently."

A rush of colour floods her cheeks. "Oh, no! I never thought of that!"

"Exactly. So he has to wonder if maybe you have a lover. Or more than one."

"But he can't think that. I don't! That's crazy."

"I know it is, and you know it is — but think how it looks to him. If I were in his shoes, that's how I'd be thinking. And to a man, that can take the edge of things. It takes a pretty experienced lady to be cool enough to start handing out condoms at, shall we refer to it as, a delicate moment?"

"Oh, Tim. Now I *am* embarrassed. Is that what he thinks?"

"Cushla, I've no idea what he thinks. But I know what I'd think. And I don't imagine he's all that different. The big question now is, what do you want to do about it? Do you want to go back to him? Have a fling with him? Or what?"

"Tim, I've only seen him half a dozen times since Lissy ... since we lost Lissy. Just to sort things out. Yesterday was the first time we did anything special together. The first time we weren't just looking after unfinished business."

"Did you enjoy being with him?"

She thinks carefully before answering. "Yes, I did. But one day doesn't make reconciliation. It was just a casual, friendly day."

"Possibly, but you know what friendship can lead to."

"Not *all* friendships lead to that."

"No, you're right there," Tim says, rising to his feet. He continues talking as he clears their tea things off the table. "You must have given him some sort of encouragement ... or at least it must have seemed like encouragement to him. You have to admit there's a big step between feeding him dinner and passing him a condom. Something must have happened that made him feel his attentions might be accepted."

Ellen picks up the milk jug and places it in the fridge, her face carefully averted. "No, I can't honestly figure out how we ended up in that situation. He was putting his clothes back on ..."

"Putting them on or taking them off?"

"No, putting them on. They got all wet when he took a shower, so I put them in the washer and dryer while we had dinner."

"You're not telling me he was sitting there buck naked?"

"No. He had a towel wrapped around him. And one of my old sweatshirts. But it was all perfectly innocent."

"Think back a few years. What would you have said if your daughter came home from a date with a story like that?"

Ellen laughs. "I guess I'd have grounded her and told her she was pretty dumb to put herself in a position like that."

"I imagine that's what most parents would do. So now you've got to figure out what you want to do about him. Do you want to ground yourself? Do you want to see him again? I can't tell you what to do. All I can do is ask questions."

"Tim, you're the most amazing man I've ever met. And one of the best friends I've ever had. I can't even imagine talking like this with anyone else."

Impulsively, she gives him a hug.

"Easy now. How do you know I won't get the wrong idea too?"

She answers with another hug. "Because you don't have any wrong ideas."

"Well, that's where you're wrong. I do have wrong ideas. Only at the time, they usually seem like right ideas."

"But not about me."

"You're a woman, aren't you? And I'm a man."

"You're not serious," Ellen says, withdrawing her arm. He seems not to notice as, smoothly, and easily, he cradles her to himself.

"Ah, but I am serious. And there's many a wrong idea I've had about you over the past months. Only they seemed like very *right* ideas. And very nice ideas. But I wasn't sure how you felt about it. Whether I was only someone to have a cup of tea and a gossip with — or whether we could enjoy something more."

Somehow, his arms are around her, his hands moving over her back, pressing him against his hips, folding the small of her back toward him. His voice is low, but she hears every word clearly.

"Now it's your turn. You've to tell me whether or not you've ever had thoughts about me."

— 13 —

TIM'S WORDS ECHO IN her ears. She doesn't know what to say. She's confused, upset, floundering. Stammering, she tries to ease out of his arms.

"I … I don't know what to say, Tim. I haven't thought about us … *like that*."

Mercifully, he turns her loose, reaching out to pluck a Kleenex from its box.

"Here, Cushla. Wipe your face. Blow your nose. It's all right. It's not the end of the world. 'Tis the end of nothin' at all. Sure it might even be the beginning. We're still friends."

Ellen giggles in spite of herself. His Irish accent comes and goes, depending on his mood. When he's teasing it comes to the fore. When he's serious, it disappears.

"I thought that was a famous last line — let's still be friends." She hiccups.

"Indeed." The word comes out in-*dayd*. "But just because it's famous, and just because it's in the movies, doesn't mean it can't be true. Sometimes it means just what it says. When you like someone well enough to enjoy their company on whatever terms they choose to give it."

During the long and sleepless hours of the night that follows, Ellen reviews what happened. Has she led him on? Has she some-how let him think she was looking for a partner? He's offered himself. Ellen hasn't exactly turned him down, but she wasn't very encouraging, either. How deeply has she hurt his feelings?

She values Tim more than she'd realized. But she's so confused. All these months, she was so sure he was gay. That made him safe, and comfortable. But what made her think that?

The memory of last night embarrasses her. First, because she's never had sex offered so casually; second, because she doesn't know what to do about it. Her mind runs like a caged squirrel, going around and around and getting nowhere.

What happened to dating, and courtship, and all those things she took for granted when she was younger? Or has Tim been courting her all along and she just didn't realize it? And yet, and yet. Watch any television show. Read any book. Sex is common currency today. People do go to bed on the first date. By modern standards, Tim has been remarkably patient. But she's not modern. The more she thinks of it, the more confused she becomes.

She remembers when she first met Tim. The first time they had a genuine conversation. He assured her he wasn't looking for a relationship, didn't he? Ellen tries to remember his exact words, but she can't. Somehow, she got the idea that he wasn't interested in sex. At least not in her sex. But tonight he'd said something else.

"I'm not a monk."

Ellen lets her mind play with the notion of Tim as a lover. He's kind. He's gentle. She likes being with him. It would probably be wonderful. But is that what she wants? Just a casual relationship?

Part of her pulls back, like the Victorian maiden threatened with a "fate worse than death." Another part of her edges forward, thinking how enjoyable it might be. It's something she's missed since the divorce.

Does she have enough gumption to call Tim and say, "Let's make a date."

If she did say yes to Tim, would that be so wrong? People don't have to be married to have sex. But still.

She's terribly confused and doesn't know what to do. She has no one to talk to. Certainly not Jennifer, Robby, or Geoff, although all three of them have likely had romantic encounters, or relationships, or whatever they call them these days. Joanne is married. That puts her in a different category, but even so, Ellen doesn't want to know what went on before Joanne's marriage. Nor does she want to discuss this with Joanne. Daughter or no daughter, married or not, this isn't fodder for a mother-daughter conversation. At least, not this mother-daughter combination.

Not for the first time, Ellen fervently wishes for a close friend. Someone she can talk to.

She does have a friend.

Tim.

The night finally ends and Ellen drags herself through the getting up process: shower, dress, breakfast. She opts for the one thing that always helps — her bike. It's cloudy, but not yet cold. Hopefully the showers in the forecast will hold off for a while. She hurries her preparations, more concerned with getting out of the building before Tim is up and about than she is by the prospect of getting caught in the rain.

The Fates are kind. He's nowhere to be seen, and there's nothing ahead of her but the road. Miles of blessed road. Tension seeps from her neck and shoulders. She imagines it strung out behind her like some grey, ephemeral mist, clinging to odd bits of shrubbery. Once again the road sings to her, humming beneath her tires. The wind whistles an obbligato through her spokes.

The sky becomes a darker grey, and in the distance, rain hangs in sheets below the clouds, not yet reaching the ground but stretching long fingers toward it. The storm is moving rapidly. She turns and heads for home. The ride is exciting now. It's a race, with the rumble of thunder spurring her on. Cars drive by, windows tightly closed, passengers lolling comfortably against their seats. People on the bus concentrate on newspapers, or look out the window with non-seeing eyes. The wind picks up, driving in little gusts and spurts, swirling leaves and dust along the surface of the road. Ellen squints, trying to keep out the grit and road dust, and pedals even harder. It's an exhilarating feeling. Primordial. Fleeing from an oncoming storm, knowing that somewhere a sheltered cave offers refuge.

The first spatter of raindrops hits the ground as she turns into the driveway. For no reason at all, she begins to laugh. She's won.

Entering the building is no longer the chore it once was. There were secrets after all, and she's mastered them.

Moments later the bike is back in its regular spot and she's wiping away any trace of road dirt and grime. It sits on its own square of carpet, bought at the flea market especially for this purpose. It's the only carpet in the apartment.

Once the bike is clean, it's Ellen's turn, and she lunges into the shower, scrubbing vigorously with a loofah, then revelling in her vanilla-scented shampoo and conditioner. She's warm, clean, dressed in fresh clothing and ready to attack breakfast when the phone rings.

"Mom, it's me."

Joanne. Her heart tightens at the sound of her daughter's voice. There's a leaden quality to it. They go through their ritual greetings before Joanne reveals the reason for her call. She and Stan have separated.

"We need a little time apart," she says. "I don't know if it's going to be permanent or not, but I've got to get away for a while. Can I come and stay with you?"

"Of course," Ellen agrees. "When will you be here?"

"On Friday."

"What time does your flight arrive?"

"I'm not flying. I thought we could drive. It'll give me time to think." She pauses. "Here. Jana wants to talk to you."

Jana is her usual sweet self, full of enthusiasm about coming to visit Grandma. They chat for a few minutes before Joanne takes the phone again.

"Thanks, Mom. You're a sweetheart."

They make their goodbyes and Ellen flies around the apartment, trying to assess what needs to be done. Joanne and Jana can share her bed and she'll get a cot for herself. She looks at the table, huddled against the wall. Another chair, too. What else? Nothing. At least, not right away. It depends on how long Joanne stays. And how things go.

She wheels her bike off of its rug and takes it to the underground storage unit.

"Sorry," she says, feeling as though she is abandoning a child.

She makes a quick trip to a nearby department store for a folding cot (she promises herself it will come in handy for future visitors), an extra chair, and a booster seat. It takes a few minutes to find a cab, but she's soon home again, tidying up the apartment and putting things away. It feels like her mother is coming to visit. She knows Joanne won't inspect the apartment or judge her housekeeping, but there's still a compulsion to make everything perfect. She's reminded of all the little projects she's put off, all the decorating she hasn't gotten around to.

Before long her stomach reminds her she hasn't yet had breakfast and it's well past lunchtime. She gives the fridge a hasty going over.

"Oh, Lord."

There's not much in there. Not much for two adults and even less for Jana.

She throws together a sandwich and eats with one hand while scribbling a shopping list with the other: Eggs. Cereal.

What kind does Jana like?

She doesn't know. Maybe better to wait until they get here and she can take Jana to the store to get something special.

Bread, milk, something for dinner Friday night. Spaghetti. It's easy. A loaf of French bread. Better get some salad stuff. Dessert — ice cream for Jana? What's her favourite flavour? Put it on a separate list with the cereal and let her choose her own. Better add some fruit. Oranges? Apples? Maybe she prefers bananas? Ellen adds *fruit* to the Jana list.

The days rush by ruthlessly and she's caught in currents she can't cope with. The rain pelts down and she wishes she could stay indoors where it's warm and dry.

As the week flies by she becomes more and more frantic. The lists pile up and the chores are never-ending. It's almost bedtime and she hasn't eaten dinner. She scrambles two eggs and sits on the couch, spooning them into her mouth while she watches TV, but she can't concentrate. The sound of a fork scraping against a bare plate tells her she's finished her eggs and toast, but she doesn't remember eating them. There was jam on the toast, but she didn't taste it. The faces on the TV screen mouth words, but she doesn't hear them. She snaps the set off and gets ready for bed.

※

Ellen wakes early the next morning, her head still full of the list of things she wants to accomplish. Too suddenly, there's a knock on the door. As she opens it, Jana launches herself into the room and leaps into Ellen's arms.

"Gramma!"

Joanne stands behind Jana, wearing a backpack, carrying a suitcase and holding Jana's favourite teddy bear in front of her.

"Hi, Mom. I'd hug you too but it would have to be a bear hug."

Joanne and her puns, Ellen thinks, nuzzling her granddaughter as she smiles at her daughter. "Okay, pumpkin," she tells Jana, lowering her to the ground. "Time for you to grow feet and walk."

Ellen takes the bear from Joanne and claims her hug.

Jana looks around, then turns to Ellen.

"When can we go to your house, Gramma?"

"You're at my house," Ellen replies.

Jana shakes her head. "No, we're not. I want to go to your *really* house."

Ellen looks at Joanne and raises her eyebrow. Embarrassed, Joanne bends down to her daughter.

"This is where Grandma lives now, honey. I told you she was in her new house."

Jana shakes her head again. "No," she says firmly. "This isn't Gramma's house."

Joanne takes Jana into her arms. "It's okay, honey. Grandma moved out of her old house and this is where she lives now. I haven't been here either. Won't it be fun to explore her new place?"

✳

It seems as though years have passed by the time they finish dinner and Jana is tucked into bed.

"Mom, I'm so confused right now. I don't know what to do."

"I know, Joanne, but it isn't something someone else can decide for you. It's your life and you have to do what's best for you. You and Jana. All I can say is take your time and don't do anything irrevocable."

"I've been thinking about this for a long time. Even before Lissy …" the words trail off.

"Have you and Stan considered counselling?"

"He doesn't want to go."

"You can go by yourself."

The silence tells Ellen this isn't going to be an option.

Joanne takes a deep breath. "Mom, I'm so confused right now. I just need to get away for a while. Everything in the house reminds me of Lissy. Everything I look at brings back memories. And I don't know where Stan's coming from — it's as though it's okay to grieve for a little while, but as far as he's concerned, that time is up and we should just get on with our lives."

Ellen waits before she replies, choosing her words carefully.

"You know you're welcome to stay here, but it can't be a permanent solution."

Joanne nods, dropping her gaze to the floor. Her response is a whisper. "I know. It's just for a little while, until I've had a chance to think."

She finishes drying the dishes and carefully places the dish towel on its rack, smoothing the folds into pleats.

"What was it like when you and Dad broke up? Was it this hard? How did you decide when to go? You've been through all this. Tell me what to do."

"We were different," she begins, then pauses. "I don't know what your father has told you, but he left first." Joanne's eyes widen. "I had no idea that was coming. It took me by surprise."

Surprise. That's an interesting word to use. Thinking back, it was more than just surprise, it was the end of a way of life, although she didn't know it at that time. Nor does she need to share that part of it with Joanne.

"He had a lawyer. I didn't. His lawyer told him to keep the house. It was in his name anyway. His lawyer set the whole thing up for him."

She pauses, nervously picking at a ragged fingernail. "I was angry. Hurt and angry. I wasn't being very logical, practical, or smart at the time."

"Did you know about her, about Verna, before?"

Ellen shrugs. "No. But she didn't break up the marriage. I know that now, but it took a while to realize the truth. It was broken long before she came along. That was the hard part, finding out that it had been over for so long and I didn't know it."

A desultory conversation bridges the next few minutes, then Joanne excuses herself. "It's been a long day and I'm really bushed. Do you mind if I turn in now?"

"Go ahead, honey. I'll stay up a while longer. I've still got a few things to do."

"G'nite, Mom," Joanne says, tiptoeing into the bedroom so as not to disturb Jana.

It reminds Ellen of a hundred nights during Joanne's growing up years. It seems so long ago. Life was so much simpler then and so much brighter for both of them.

✳

Tim calls the next day. "Got time for a cuppa?"

"Sorry, Tim. Joanne and Jana got in yesterday and I'm not sure what their plans are for today."

"Anything I can do? Friendly shoulder required?"

Ellen laughs. "I'd love to talk, and a friendly shoulder is always welcome, but I can't tell you when I'll be free."

"You can always bring them over here for a visit. I can draw funny pictures for the little one."

"Thanks, Tim. Give me a day to find out what their plans are."

It turns out Joanne and Jana want to see Al, so Ellen arranges for them to go there the next afternoon. Jana's a bit apprehensive.

"Does Grampa still live in a really house?" she asks.

"He certainly does," Joanne replies.

Baby tears shimmer across Jana's eyes. "I don't like things always changing. Lissy went away and Daddy went away and Gramma doesn't live in a really house and everything is all muddled up."

Joanne scoops the little girl up in her arms.

"I'm here, honey. I'll always be here. Daddy still loves you. He loves you very, very much. And Grandma isn't any different just because she's living in a different place. Nothing has changed. Not the important things. We all love you. That's all you have to remember."

Jana ducks her head, then peeks up and smiles at her mother. She's restless and wriggles in Joanne's arms, eager to escape their confining grasp.

"Jana," Ellen says, "I need you to help me. I have to go to the store for some cereal, but I don't know what kind to get. Any ideas?"

"Super Frankenstein's. That's the bestest one."

"Does Mommy like that kind of cereal?"

While Jana nods an enthusiastic yes, Joanne grasps her throat with both hands and makes a strangling sound.

Ellen smiles.

"So, what's your next favourite? Maybe something that Mommy likes too?"

Jana's forehead puckers in a frown. "I don't know."

"Tell you what, let's go to the store and see what they have. Maybe that will help you make up your mind."

The shopping trip is a splendid diversion. It takes endless time to choose Jana's favourite cereal, favourite fruit, and favourite drink. Picking her favourite fruit evolves into a game of identifying shapes and colours. Eventually she chooses red flame grapes, because, as she explains, "they crunch."

Over breakfast the next morning, Joanne discusses her plans for the day.

"Did you want to come over to Dad's place with me?" she asks, casually.

The words are a slap: "Dad's place." How easily it's become Dad's place. What happened to all years it was my place, too, Ellen wonders.

"Please, Gramma," Jana interjects.

"No, pumpkin." She turns to Joanne. "I'd rather let you and Jana have some time together with him. I have a few other things that I have to do. That reminds me." She reaches across the counter. "Here, I had a key made for you so you can come and go as you please."

Five minutes after they leave, Ellen is in her biking togs and headed for the underground storage to reclaim her bike. She feels she should apologize for leaving it there. Moments later she's on the road, pedalling as hard as she can while her mind goes into high gear, trying to focus on Joanne and her problem, trying to decide how to help her, trying not to think of what is happening at this moment in "Dad's place."

It's a beautiful day, one of the respite days fall offers before winter settles in. Trees flaunt their leaves, flowing in colourful clouds as the wind plucks them from their branches. There's a last brave show in the gardens as chrysanthemums break into billowing cushions of blooms. Large mums, shaggy mums, and little button mums join the late-blooming glads and the end-of-the-season burst of begonias and geraniums. Impatiens have reached their maximum growth and leggy alyssum fills every crevice of borders and beds, scenting the air with a perfume that reminds Ellen of the sachets her mother tucked into her lingerie drawer. There's a symphony of colour and a cornucopia of smells. Wood smoke and burning leaves challenge the scent of freshly cut grass as gardeners get ready for the rainy season ahead.

When she returns to her apartment, the phone is ringing.

"Mom, it's me. Joanne."

Ellen laughs to herself. *Does she think I can't recognize her voice?*

"Dad's got tons of photo albums and things he wants me go to through and I was thinking it might be easier to stay here for a while. Jana and I can sleep in my old room. There's really a lot of stuff that needs to be gone through, so I thought we could spend today and tomorrow here. Would you mind?"

"Of course not. I thought you might want to do something of the sort."

"Thanks, Mom. I'll be over in a while to pick up some of our things." She giggles into the phone. "I don't think any of my old clothes I left here would still fit me — and I know they won't fit Jana. I'll phone before I leave."

"No need. Just come. You have the key in case I'm out."

She uses the unexpected day to get in another ride, cleaning her bike thoroughly before once again returning it to the basement storage locker.

As she re-enters her apartment, the phone rings. This time it's Tim.

"Got a minute to talk? Just wondered how things were going."

The turmoil that had evaporated during her ride swirls back again. What to tell Tim? Why not be honest and tell him the truth? She has no idea where this relationship is going. She enjoys his company but she's not sure if she wants to go beyond that point. What if it doesn't work out? She might lose his friendship, and at this moment she realizes she values that above anything else. But it's hard to say any of this over the phone.

"Got lots of time. Joanne and Jana went to see Al and they're staying with him for a couple of days."

There's a pause before he replies.

"I was just going to make myself something to drink. Care to come over and share?"

"I'll be right there."

Conversation flows easily with Tim. She finds herself telling him about Joanne and Stan's problems, about her concerns for Jana, about Joanne's anger.

"Stan doesn't know how to cope with her anger," Ellen explains. "I've noticed it before. He usually just lets her do whatever she wants, but this time he seems to be taking a stand of some sort, but it doesn't seem to be the right one. I don't know what to say to either of them."

"Counselling?" Tim asks.

"No. Neither one thinks they need it."

Tim moves behind her, placing his hands on her shoulders and massaging them gently. "It's hard, isn't it, to stand back and watch someone you care about go through something like this." As though talking to himself, he continues, "Even harder when you want to help and there's nothing you can do."

Abruptly, he withdraws his hands.

"I've got a truly goofy video — the best of the Super Bowl commercials over the years. They're always good to watch and it's more fun to laugh with someone than to laugh alone. Want to watch it with me?"

They settle comfortably on the sofa and he starts the video. He's right. They are funny. They sit laughing together, after it ends, recalling favourite moments. Somehow, his arm is around her and she's nestled into the curve of his shoulder. It feels good. She's missed the intimate feel of a masculine hug, the bristly scrape of an end-of-the-day kiss. And the feeling of warmth and wanting that suffuses her as their embrace grows more heated.

Somehow, his hands are possessing her, moving her, undoing clothing.

This can't be happening, her mind whispers.

Ellen knows she should resist, but she doesn't want to. Her body needs and wants what's happening. He scoops her into his arms and lifts her from the sofa.

"We'll do this right," he says, "in a comfortable bed."

She knows she should say something, but all she can do is smile as he carries her into the bedroom.

"I've been waiting for this," Tim tells her, as he lowers her gently onto the duvet.

"For what?" she murmurs.

"For us," he replies.

Suddenly he turns and moves to the door.

"Where are you going?"

"We need wine and candles," he announces.

Moments later he's back with a bottle of Kahlua and a large candle, whose flame flickers as he walks.

"Now," he whispers, "let's play."

The bottle gives a comfortable glug as he tips it, pours a little in his palm and smoothes it onto her breast.

"What are you doing?" She laughs. "You're wasting good Kahlua!"

"It's only wasted if I don't make use of it," he responds, lowering his head and touching her breast with his tongue.

"Hmm. Tasty." He grins.

"What a goof you are."

"We'll see about that."

He drizzles a few more drops of Kahlua onto her breast. Her nipple rises, swelling with need. He takes her into his mouth, bringing back a long-forgotten desire deep within her. She turns to him, but he gently pushes her shoulders back.

"Not yet, Cushla," he says. "You're a beautiful woman and I want you as I've never wanted another woman. I want you as a stag wants a doe, as an eagle wants its mate, and as a man wants a woman. And I shall have you that way."

Abruptly he rolls her onto her stomach and straddles her, locking her hips between strong thighs as he pulls her toward him. She senses his heat before she feels him. His fingers busy themselves, massaging her, lubricating her, teasing her, before he slides gently into her, then moves more harshly and strongly as the rhythm of the moment catches them.

"Like a stag, like a stag," he chants. "Like a wild stag in the forest."

Like the doe, she encourages him, urging him deeper. At last he comes in a surge of heat and power. She moves, trying to ease away, but he holds her firmly.

"That was the first. Now I want you as an eagle wants its mate."

"An eagle?"

"Aye, an eagle. Strong, free, and powerful. Come."

He stands, then extends his hand.

"But what do eagles do?"

"They fly to the highest point they can reach," Tim explains, whirling her around in a dizzy embrace. "Then, when they can fly no higher, they face each other, like this." He turns her toward himself and locks her in closely. "You don't have wings, but wrap your legs around my waist. Hold tightly now. We're high in the air."

Ellen leaps upward, hands on his shoulders, cinching her legs around his waist.

Abruptly he stiffens, groans, and fends her off.

"Jesus bloody Christ woman! Think like an eagle, not a gorilla. You're breaking my back."

He pauses, catching his breath. Ellen freezes in confusion. He shakes his head, then smiles at her.

"It's all right. My back goes out sometimes. You caught me off balance. That's all. Let's try it again. Only this time, don't leap on me."

As he lifts her gently, she twines herself around him, clutching tightly while his hands slide beneath her buttocks.

"And now he takes her."

Swiftly, he enters her, moving her to match the thrust of his hips. And explosive moment later, he slides his hands under her arms, and gently lowers her down.

"Then just before they reach the ground, they break apart and fly away. 'Tis a beautiful sight to see, and an even greater thing to enjoy."

They move slowly to the bed. Her knees are trembling and her desire is mounting. She needs this man. Needs to feel him deep inside her. Needs to hold him so tightly he becomes part of her, his image pressed into her flesh.

"And now, Cushla, I want you as a man wants a woman."

They clasp each other, but eager as she is, he doesn't enter her yet. His tongue explores her body, travelling through the cleft between her breasts, visiting her navel, then reaching for her innermost core. Pressure pounds throughout her body. She wants him, needs him. Now. But still he teases. Gently he nuzzles until she can contain herself no longer.

"For God's sake, Tim, no more!"

He raises himself, moving upward, and she glances down to look at him. She's never seen a man so large, nor so erect. Slowly he advances, sliding himself into her. Then harder and faster he presses against her innermost being. She gives herself to the moment, feels him filling her, expanding until he is part of her. She can wait no longer. There is a blessed moment of release, like breakers crashing on the sand, like lightning in a summer storm — all the clichés she can remember sudden seem fresh again. He laughs as she comes, and only then allows himself release.

"And that is the way a man takes a woman." He smiles.

They nuzzle together, spent, needing each other's warmth and the gentleness that comes after.

"Come," he says, leading her to the shower, where they take turns washing each other, then drying one another off.

They cuddle again, lying close together on the bed. Gradually she hears the traffic noises diminish. She's lulled, ready to sleep, when suddenly she remembers Joanne and looks at the bedside clock. It's one thirty in the morning.

"Tim, I've got to go home."

"You're welcome to spend the night," he says.

"No, I've got to get back to my own place. I don't know when Joanne is going to phone in the morning, but I have to be there."

"Are you sure?"

She's sure. Quickly she dresses and Tim walks her to the door. "I can't escort you home like this," he laughs, gesturing at his naked body.

He grabs her for a lusty kiss, then grins. "Now I definitely can't walk outside," he says, looking down at an erection that is beginning to happen.

"You're insatiable." She laughs.

"No, I'm Irish," he retorts.

Ellen blows him a kiss and walks to her own apartment.

Not until she is about to climb into bed does she realize Tim didn't wear a condom and she laughs at the incongruity of asking her ex-husband to wear one while her friend makes love to her three times in one night without. Abruptly she stops laughing. Unprotected sex isn't funny. She's sure now that he's not gay, but equally sure that he's had other partners — many other partners.

Now she has a new set of worries.

— 14 —

JOANNE AND JANA TUMBLE into the apartment early the next morning, twin whirlwinds exploding into Ellen's world. Jana's words roll from her in a torrent as she simultaneously tries to struggle out of her coat, untie her shoes, give Ellen a hug, and show off her newest treasure. Joanne is only slightly better as she balances an armload of bags and boxes while helping Jana.

"Let me give you a hand with those," Ellen says, deftly grabbing the load from Joanne's arms.

"Mom, we had the most wonderful visit. It was great to see Dad again." There was a short pause. "He sends his love."

She waits for a reaction that doesn't materialize.

"Grampa gave me a picture of mommy when she was little," Jana chirps, waving a snapshot in front of Ellen's face.

She remembers it well. The girls' fifth birthday. She had pointed at something to distract their attention while Al sneaked behind their backs, a puppy cradled in each arm. The pups wore party hats and big ribbon bows.

"I still remember how I felt at that moment." Joanne laughs.

"How, Mommy?"

"I couldn't believe what I was seeing. Total shock! That was probably the happiest moment of my life." She bends down and hugs Jana. "Until you came along, munchkin."

Jana is off and running with a thousand new questions. What were the puppies' names? Where did they stay? Did they sleep on her bed? Where were they now?

Joanne solemnly relates the history of the pups — funny things they did, exasperating moments, special memories. Then, of course, comes the loaded question.

"Can I get a puppy, Mommy?"

Joanne glances at her mother.

"We'll have to see, sweetheart."

"That means no," Jana says, pouting.

"No, it just means we can't get one right now. Things are a little confused right now. We'll have to wait a while."

"Does that mean I can?"

"Maybe later."

"You didn't say maybe. You said wait a while. How long is a while?"

Ellen fiddles with her fingers, smoothing a cuticle, ignoring Joanne's silent plea for help. The obvious answer is yes, if they go back home and she patches things up with Stan. And no if she moves into an apartment and goes out to work every day.

"Well, a while doesn't have any real time to it. It's not like tomorrow."

"Is it next week?"

"No, not then, either."

"Before my birthday?"

Joanne doesn't answer.

"When we go home?" Jana persists.

"Jana, leave it." A tinge of anger colours Joanne's voice. "We've got lots of other things to think about before we worry about a puppy. But I'll make you a promise. You will have a puppy one day. Okay?"

"Is that a really truly promise?"

"It is."

Amazingly, Jana is satisfied. As Joanne turns to look at her mother, Ellen can't help but think how much the two look alike. The same wide open eyes, the same small, neat chin, the same pleading expression.

"Dad would really like to see you again."

Ellen takes a deep breath.

"Joanne, leave it. I've got lots of other things to think about. Okay?"

Even as the words slip past her lips, she wants to recall them. Joanne's eyes react as though she's been slapped. And of course, by repeating her own words, Ellen has slapped her — verbally — but it's just as painful as a physical slap.

"I'm sorry, honey. I'm not upset with you. It's your father. It isn't fair of him to use you like that. He knows how I feel. He's just not willing to accept it."

"Well, at least you didn't promise me I could have a new daddy one day." She tries to laugh off her mother's comment.

"Joanne, you already have a father. That doesn't change. It never will."

"I know, Mom, but this seems so wrong. He's miserable living by himself, and you're miserable living by yourself."

"Whoa! Who says I'm miserable?"

"Sorry, that's the wrong word. I should have said lonesome."

"Not even lonesome."

"But you don't have any friends here."

"You're wrong. I do. You simply don't know them. Believe me, Joanne. I have a very full and satisfying life without your father. And I plan to keep it that way. Now can we please change the subject?"

As if on cue, the phone rings. It's Stan, for Joanne. As Ellen hands over the phone, Joanne gestures toward Jana. Ellen nods.

"Come on, honey. I've got a new book that I think you'll like."

Joanne's voice follows them as they walk into the bedroom to look at the book, a story about a caterpillar whose multi-legged adventures carry him to strange and wonderful places. When the story ends, Jana considers for a moment before turning to Ellen.

"That wasn't really, was it, Gramma?"

"No, pumpkin, that was make believe."

Jana's face reflects the turmoil in her mind. It's like watching a little rivulet, twisting its way down a rainy windowpane, darting first one way, then another, reaching toward ever larger globules of water, only running true when it becomes large enough to resist their pull.

"Mommy used to tell me things that were really, but now she says things that are make believe, only she thinks they're really."

"Mommy's having a hard time right now, munchkin. You'll just have to be patient with her."

Jana looks up solemnly, large, round eyes fixed on Ellen. Then she sighs and looks away. Ellen isn't sure if Jana thinks she's in league with her mother, or whether adults simply can't be trusted anymore.

At that moment, Joanne appears in the doorway.

"Hey, guys. I've got a great idea. Let's go down to the mall for ice cream."

It's obvious she wants to talk, but needs something to distract Jana. Baskin and Robbins and their 31 flavours might do it. By this time, Ellen's curiosity is aroused, but she's also resentful of Joanne's easy assumption that she has nothing else to do. Wickedly, she wonders what might happen if she told her daughter she had a date with her lover later on today, or wanted to go on a fifty-mile bike ride. It's a beautiful day, perfect for riding, and Ellen would far rather be doing that than wandering around in the mall, but curiosity wins and she agrees to go.

It's an easy venue for talking. Jana is distracted by sidewalk displays — toy shops, a pet shop, a book store. The activity centre interests her but she isn't feeling confident enough to leave her mother's side to investigate. She watches for a while, then they resume their stroll and arrive at the ice cream store, where Jana flits like a hummingbird from one choice to another. Eventually she settles on rainbow and they seat themselves on a nearby bench.

"Jana, you can watch the puppies while you eat your ice cream," Joanne says, and as Jana scampers to the pet shop window, she turns to Ellen.

"Dad offered to take Jana for a few days so Stan and I can go somewhere and spend some uninterrupted time together to talk things over. He thought neutral ground might make it easier."

"Knowing your father, he's probably fantasizing a second honeymoon for you and Stan."

Joanne shrugs.

"Whatever. Stan and I need to talk. Putting it off just makes it that much more difficult. Maybe Dad's right; neutral ground might make a difference. We certainly couldn't do it at home and it's time we got things resolved. It's wearing me down ... and I know it's upsetting Jana, too."

The waltzing finally comes to an end as she faces Ellen and takes her hand.

"Mom, just for the weekend, could you move back in with Dad?"

Ellen's eyes widen in shock.

"Could I what?"

"Well, it's hard for him to look after Jana by himself. He's not used to little kids. And it's just for the weekend. He's not asking you to make any long-term commitment ... or any commitment at all. Just to spend the weekend there. Please, Mom?"

Ellen locks her jaw to prevent words from spilling out of her mouth, takes a deep breath, than another, before she trusts herself to reply.

"Joanne, I think it's a great idea for you and Stan to talk. It's a wonderful idea to have your talk on neutral ground. But it's not a good idea for me to play house with your father for the weekend. If you'd feel more comfortable, leave Jana with me. I'm used to looking after little kids. I've had some experience, remember? Or leave Jana with him. He's capable enough. He's had some experience too."

Joanne studies the nail on her left thumb, examining it closely before she speaks.

"Okay, so he wants to spend some time with you. Is that so wrong? Wouldn't it be great if you could resolve your differences with him and Stan and I could sort things out too?"

"And live happily ever after?" Ellen adds.

Joanne scrutinizes her other thumbnail.

"Joanne, your father is a manipulator. He's using you and he's using Jana to make me do something I don't want to do. Something I'm not going to do. I spent thirty years dancing to his whims, walking a tightrope so as not to upset him or send him off into one of his moods, or generate a tantrum.

"No, Joanne. I will not spend a weekend with your father."

"Even if …"

"Even if nothing. I won't do it. Jana can stay with me. She'd be happy. Your father can visit if he wants to spend some time with her. But that's it. Or you can leave her with him."

Angry as she is, Ellen has to stifle laughter as Joanne tries to marshal an argument. Her daughter is once again the twelve-year-old who is convinced she has the meanest mother in the world because she isn't allowed to do something that "everyone else" is doing.

"Joanne, forget it. Whatever you were about to say, forget it."

The stony silence is accompanied by a pair of glaring eyes.

Ellen walks to the pet shop window and kneels beside Jana.

"Which one is your favourite?"

Jana has no trouble making up her mind.

"That one. The little brown one with the spots on his nose. I like him."

Joanne has walked over toward them.

Ellen extends an olive branch.

"Which one is your favourite, Joanne?"

Joanne refuses to accept it.

"Is there anything we need in the mall, or can we go home now?"

"Home is fine," Ellen replies, levelly.

Jana and Ellen make most of the conversation on the ride home, choosing names for some of the puppies. They continue their conversation during the tense dinner. Ellen continues to chat with her granddaughter while Joanne steps out in the hall to make a series of phone calls on her cell. Finally, it's bedtime for Jana. Ellen runs the water into the tub and laces it with bubble bath. She builds bubble hats on Jana's head and makes bubble animals until the water begins to cool. Then it's time to rub her dry with a thick, warm towel and pop her into her pyjamas.

Joanne re-enters the apartment.

"Mom, I've been thinking."

Ellen waits, while Joanne chooses her words.

"I really need time to work things out with Stan. And Jana needs to spend time with her grandfather, too. If you won't help Dad, he'll just have to cope the best he can. After all, he did help raise four children. He can't be *that* inept."

Words rise to Ellen's lips. Can't he? Where was he when....? But there's no point to that now. She bites off her response. Whatever Joanne's memories are, they won't change now, regardless of what Ellen may or may not say.

"I'm sure he'll do just fine. When will Jana visit with him?"

"This weekend."

The words hang between them. Ellen throws Joanne a small gift.

"Tell him to call me if he needs help."

Joanne relaxes and Ellen stifles a smile. It's so easy to read her daughter's face. At this moment, Joanne is confident that things will go according to her plan. Al will call, Ellen will rush to his aid, they'll realize they miss each other, and like a sudden burst of sunshine after a storm, everything will be well again.

It's a classic response to a classic situation. Only it doesn't usually happen after the child of a divorce approaches thirty. Or does it? Is it something children yearn for no matter how old they are? At this point it seems Joanne is more interested in getting her parents back together than in solving the problems in her own marriage.

It will make a funny story to share with Tim, when this is all over.

The next day, she helps Jana load her backpack with the things she'll need for her sleepover at Grandpa's.

"Can Grampa make braids?" Jana asks, trying to decide which of her hair clips and bows she wants to take with her.

"I don't know," Ellen replies. "I don't think he's ever tried."

"But I like to wear braids."

"You're not wearing them now," Ellen points out.

Joanne peers out from Jana's eyes.

Ellen sighs.

"How would it be if I do your hair in braids before you go?"

Jana considers briefly, then smiles. Her world is serene again.

— 15 —

SUNDAY IS SUCH A beautiful day that it catches Ellen by surprise. It unfolds with a wonderful sense of freedom. Jana and Joanne are away. She is answerable to no one. The drizzle of the past few days has ended and sunlight streams through the window, a marker of Indian summer. Breakfast can wait. Coffee can wait. Everything can wait while she takes advantage of this unexpected gift.

The liberating sound of wheels against the road frees her mind and she turns her thoughts to Joanne and Stan, and to Al. Joanne has shown more backbone than she herself ever had, and that's a big plus in Ellen's mind. Still, she knows how manipulative Al can be. From his point of view, it would be comfortable to have Joanne move home to stay. She'd keep house for him. Is he capable of being that devious? Perhaps not consciously, but yes, it's possible. It's selfish behaviour, but he likes to be comfortable.

She battles with the notion that she should warn Joanne. But warn her against her own father? It seems so unfair. She's damned if she does and damned if she doesn't. Why isn't there someone who can tell her the right answers and make decisions for her? For that matter, why can't she make decisions for herself? Why can't she stand up for herself?

The turmoil continues in her mind, fuelled by the rhythm of the road. Where did Al get off, deciding he had a right to come riding with her, whether she wanted him to or not? Deciding she should come at his beck and go through things in the house. Deciding … it didn't matter what it was, she was expected to respond. Not just respond but acquiesce. Whatever he wanted, whenever *he* wanted.

Was Tim any better? Was what happened with Tim anything more than his fantasy? Yes, she was willing, but there could have been more warning — a buildup, maybe even a date, a dinner, a prelude of some sort. It was almost rape. Very pleasant rape, but nonetheless an invasion of herself. And unprotected. That was the ultimate in selfish behaviour on his part.

And Joanne. Much as she loved her daughter, much as she wanted to help her, surely she could have said something more than a few hours before arriving on her doorstep? What if she'd been on her way to California. Or in California? What would she have done then?

The wheels and her pedals echo the metre of California.

California, California, California, like the rhythm of a steam engine as it chugs along the road.

Ah, but steam engines arrive at their destinations. And she doesn't seem to.

She should be in California already, she thinks. She should have been there some time ago. But always, something gets in the way. Something she can't say no to. Something she has to accommodate.

As she rides, she notices a lull in the traffic, cars slowing down. Curious. It doesn't seem like there's anything ahead on the road that would cause a problem. But something is happening. The cars go slower and slower and she finally catches up to some of the traffic.

She notices a woman sitting in her car, pulled over to the

side of the road. She's slumped over the steering wheel, listening to the car radio. Tears trickle down her face. The woman is in obvious distress and Ellen slows, pulling in beside the car to see if she can offer help. Ellen's shadow draws the woman's attention. Wordlessly, she gestures through the open window, shaking her head as the newscaster's voice repeats the horrifying description of a tragic incident in New York. An airplane has flown into one of the towers, hundreds of people are trapped and smoke is pouring from the rupture in the tower's façade. A second plane has flown into another tower and there are reports of other terrorist attacks against national landmarks.

"I can't believe it," the woman says.

"Is it a radio play?" Ellen suggests, unable to grasp the enormity of the event.

The woman shakes her head. "No. It's on all the stations." She listens for a moment, then continues.

"I'm so scared. I don't know what to do."

The woman stretches her hand out the window. Ellen clasps it, attempting to reassure her, but there is no reassurance anywhere.

"I have to go," Ellen says.

"I know. I do too," the woman replies.

Gently, Ellen removes her hand from the woman's grasp, mounts her bike, and retraces her route home. She has to phone Joanne and tell her not to let Jana listen to the radio or watch the TV. But when she enters her apartment, the phone is ringing. It's Al, his voice brimming with concern.

"I heard," she whispers. "It's unbelievable."

"I'm coming over," he says. "You can stay here."

Wordlessly, she shakes her head, no, but he doesn't wait for an answer.

"I'll be there in ten minutes."

He arrives even sooner, bringing Jana with him.

"We'll go back to my place," he announces, holding the car door open.

"Did she hear?" Ellen asks, nodding at Jana.

Al nods. "Yeah. I thought she was watching cartoons, but by the time I realized what was going on it was too late to shut the TV off."

"Joanne's still here," he adds. "Stan was supposed to fly out today, but all flights are cancelled."

They return to Al's house. Her house. When they arrive, Joanne gives her a quick hug, then takes Jana into the backyard while Al and Ellen watch the towers crumble again and again, seeing the stricken faces of the survivors, ghost-like in a white frisson of cement dust, the ravaged skyline raped by a terrorist hand.

In a world that moves in slow motion, they sit together, unbelieving and bewildered by the drama playing out before them. Anchors interrupt with breaking news. Additional planes have been hijacked. There are fears that further attacks will be launched against other, undefined targets. The president has been whisked away to a secure location, the vice-president to a separate bunker at an undisclosed alternate site.

Ellen feels vulnerable in a way she's never felt before — unprotected, abandoned and bewildered.

"Nothing's the same anymore, is it?" she whispers. "The world is changed."

Al places his hand on her shoulder. "You don't have to worry. I'll look after you. You know that, Babe."

She shakes free.

"No. You'd like to … just like we'd like to look after Joanne and Jana. But we can't. There aren't any more happy endings."

Al looks hurt and bewildered.

"We can look after each other," he offers.

"No, Al. I don't think we can even do that anymore. We have to look after ourselves. I have to look after myself, because there isn't anyone else I can depend on." As she speaks, she feels empty, vulnerable and insubstantial. She feels as though there has never been anyone she could depend on, but she didn't realize it until now.

He looks at her with those spaniel eyes, waiting for her to take back the hurtful words.

"I don't mean it unkindly, Al. I'm not putting you down. I'm just saying my world has changed and I've had to change with it. Now it's more important than ever."

She isn't telling the truth. She's feeling incredibly sad. Everything is being destroyed; everything she's believed in and everything she has dreamed of is being destroyed.

Then the sadness is replaced by anger, hot, roiling, burning anger. How dare they, whoever "they" are, to do this to her? To take away everyone's dreams? To destroy so wantonly the things that made her world so unique and wonderful?

Suddenly, she's tired. Tired of arguing. Tired of scraping along. Tired of getting the short end of life. Abruptly, she stands.

"Please, would you drive me home? I have things to do."

He's truly bewildered now.

"It's important," she says. "I really do have to leave. I'll go say goodbye to Joanne and Jana while you start the car."

In the backyard, she gives quick hugs.

"Joanne, I'm leaving on a trip tomorrow. I've been planning it for quite some time. I'm sorry to throw this at you at the last minute, but I can't put it off."

Before Joanne can voice objections, Ellen continues.

"You have my spare key. It's up to you whether you stay here, with your father, or whether you go back to my place and stay there. If you want my advice, you'll head back home and try to work things out with Stan. It'll never happen as long as you stay here."

"When are you coming back?" Joanne asks.

"I don't know," she replies.

"But where—"

Ellen cuts her off.

"I'll let you know later. I have to go now."

Quickly she turns, kneels down and hugs Jana tightly to her, kissing her cheek, then whirls out the gate to the driveway where Al sits, revving the engine.

"I don't get it," he complains. "What's so important that you have to rush away like this?"

"I'll tell you later," she promises.

At the apartment she rejects his offer of assistance, closes the car door firmly, and lets herself in the front door.

There's a note on the door of her apartment.

Call me when you get in. Tim.

She walks down the hall and raps quickly on his door.

"Cushla," he says, reaching for her. "I was worried about you. Where were you? Have you heard—"

"I have," she says, not moving quickly enough to avoid his grasp. She endures his hug but doesn't respond.

"What's wrong?" he asks. "Did you know someone …?" the question hangs, unfinished, in the air.

"No," she shakes her head. "No. Not that."

She takes a deep breath and looks at him squarely.

"Tim, I'll be leaving for a while. I'm going on a trip, so we won't be seeing each other."

"You'll be back." He smiles.

She says nothing.

"Where are you off to, then?" he asks.

"It's a bike trip," she says.

"A long one?"

She nods. "Yes. I don't know how long I'll be gone. As long as it takes, I guess."

She looks at him and once again sees those damned spaniel

eyes looking back at her. Does everyone in the world have those eyes? Does everyone look wounded?

"Would you be wanting some company?" His voice is charming, beguiling. *Who can resist me?* it asks.

"It isn't that kind of trip," she says. As he draws a breath, she interrupts. "I'm sorry. I don't have much time and I've got a lot to do. I just wanted to say goodbye. It's been good knowing you."

"That sounds very final."

"It isn't meant to be. It's just goodbye. That's all. I'm sorry, I have to go now."

Turning, she strides down the hall and enters her own apartment.

Tomorrow. Tomorrow she'll leave. Not necessarily for California. Not necessarily for anywhere. Just go. For as long as she needs.

She sorts things into piles: what to take, what to leave. Stuffing the bike panniers, she makes further decisions, cutting out some items, adding others.

I'm being selfish. Truly selfish, she realizes, with wonderment. *And it feels good.*

At last her packing is done. She sets out the clothing she'll wear in the morning: bike pants and jersey, a windbreaker, light socks to go with her bike shoes, a comfortable sport bra that neither bites into her ribs nor chafes under her arms. She adds a pair of boy-style briefs that won't bunch up under her crotch or rub her cheeks raw in the course of a long ride. And this will be a long ride, she promises herself.

Laughing, she dismantles her "burglar alarm" from the bathroom window, then retrieves the book and wedge from behind her bedroom door, sending them all down the trash chute in a clump that bangs its way down with a satisfying clatter.

It's past the hour when the chute should be used, as the bold faced sign reminds her, but at this moment, she doesn't care.

Not about the noise, not about the trash, not about anything but her trip.

I might die tomorrow, she acknowledges. *Or maybe the day after. Or not for fifty more years. But I'm tired of doing what's expected of me, apologizing to people and being nice whether I want to or not.*

"It's my turn now."

She steps firmly back into her apartment, closes the door behind her, and clicks the lock. Her mind is whirling as memories flash by: her mother, her poor mother, who seemed always in the background; her father and his bossy, overwhelming manner; Al, with his assumption that he always knew best; even Tim, turning her weakness to his advantage. Mentally she rages at them.

It's my turn now and no one, not a grubby bunch of terrorists or anyone else, is going to take it from me.

It's after midnight by the time she finishes putting everything away, but she's content with what she's done. Tomorrow, she'll go.

"Tomorrow," she whispers. "Tomorrow and tomorrow and tomorrow. They're all mine. And I don't have to be afraid anymore."

Smiling, she slides slowly under the covers and drifts gently into sleep.